"I want to forget our night together."

"Well, I damn well don't, Diana!" Marcus's face went white with rage. "And I think you're lying. You might want to forget that night but you can't, can you?"

"Marcus, this is ridiculous," Diana responded in panic. "I don't know why you're doing this."

"You don't?" Marcus reached out to trail his fingertips along her bare arm. "Do you remember how it felt when I touched you, Diana?" he whispered against her lips. "You want me. Just give me a chance to prove to you how good it could be between us."

"No," Diana gasped, her denial sounding weak and unconvincing even to her own ears. The touch of Marcus's hands and mouth was unbearably erotic, but it wasn't enough. She wanted more...needed more.

PENNY JORDAN was constantly in trouble in school because of her inability to stop daydreaming—especially during French lessons. In her teens she was an avid romance reader, although it didn't occur to her to try writing one herself until she was older. "My first half-dozen attempts ended up ingloriously," she remembers, "but I persevered, and one manuscript was finished." She plucked up the courage to send it to a publisher, convinced her book would be rejected. It wasn't, and the rest is history! Penny is married and lives in Cheshire.

Books by Penny Jordan

Don't miss any of our special offers. Write to us at the following address for information on our newest releases.

Harlequin Reader Service
901 Fuhrmann Blvd., P.O. Box 1397, Buffalo, NY 14240
Canadian address: P.O. Box 603,
Fort Erie, Ont. L2A 5X3

PENNY JORDAN

for one night

Harlequin Books

TORONTO • NEW YORK • LONDON
AMSTERDAM • PARIS • SYDNEY • HAMBURG
STOCKHOLM • ATHENS • TOKYO • MILAN

Harlequin Presents first edition January 1989
ISBN 0-373-11137-1

Original hardcover edition published in 1987
by Mills & Boon Limited

CHAPTER ONE

NUMB with shock, Diana moved to one side as the first spadeful of earth hit the coffin.

A long, deep shudder racked through her body as she stared down into the darkness of the open grave. In that box was the body of her best friend; for eighteen long months they had fought together against the enemy destroying Leslie's body, and less than a week ago they had lost their fight.

Even now, she could hardly believe it. She and Leslie had been at university together; they had got their degrees at the same time, and their first jobs. Then they had lost touch for several years, meeting again only when Leslie's first book had been published, and she herself had been working as a researcher for the host of the television chat show on which Leslie had been asked to appear.

To their mutual delight they had discovered that they still shared the same outlook on life, and the same zany sense of humour. Now that she could support herself as a writer, Leslie had decided to move to London, and it seemed a natural follow-on from this decison that they should buy a flat together.

Both of them had their own personal lives; Leslie was still getting over a two-year relationship that had turned sour when her lover became jealous of her writing success. And as for her own love-life ... Diana sighed.

In the days when she had first joined the television

5

company and had still been starry-eyed with wonder and excitement, she had fallen hard for one of the producers, only to learn quite by accident from one of his previous victims that he made a second career out of bemusing and seducing all the young and naïve newcomers to the company, callously notching up his tally of successes with a celebratory booze-up with his menfriends, when he regaled them with the intimate details of his amatory skills.

She had been one of the lucky ones, she had found out about him before it was too late, but it had left her with a deep mistrust of all media men. She froze them off the moment they attempted to get close to her.

Between themselves, she and Leslie had agreed that they were better off concentrating on their careers, and treating men with the same casual disregard that the male sex adopted towards women. What neither of them had realised was that there was going to be precious little time in their lives *for* socialising. Leslie had developed the first symptoms of the disease that was to kill her within weeks of them moving in together.

At first she had said nothing; but Leslie was wasting away visibly, and in the end she had been forced to tackle her friend about her loss of weight, Diana remembered.

She turned her head away from the awfulness of the gaping hole in the earth, a cruelly bitter spring wind teasing silky strands of red-gold hair and blowing them against her pale face.

She had thought that perhaps Leslie was suffering from some eating disorder; but the truth had been far worse than her imaginings.

She had been woken up one night by Leslie's heartbroken sobs, and had gone into her room. At first, Leslie had tried to deny that anything was wrong, but, finally, she had told Diana everything.

She had felt unwell for a while, tired and listless, and at first she had put it down to the strain of her broken relationship, plus the heavy workload she had taken on. She had gone to see her doctor, hoping he could recommend a tonic, only he had sent her to hospital for tests, and the results were indisputable. She had leukaemia.

They had talked long into the night; Leslie had been completely open with her about her prognosis. She had no family; the aunt and uncle who had brought her up had been killed in a plane crash while they were at university. She had decided that she would find herself a privately run hospice where she could be properly looked after, but Diana had firmly refused to countenance this.

They were friends, and they would stay friends. *She* would look after Leslie.

It had proved harder than either of them anticipated. On several occasions the doctors had wanted to keep Leslie in hospital but, knowing how great her fear and distress would be, Diana had refused to allow them to do so. She had taken Leslie home and nursed her herself. In the last dreadfully painful weeks, Diana had applied for compassionate leave from her job.

Fresh tears blurred her vision, the first she had been able to weep for her friend. Her pain and anger went beyond mere tears; it seemed incomprehensible, an enormity of unfairness and illogical wrong that Leslie should be dead. She had been so young, had had so much to give to life.

Diana shivered in the cold wind. It was April; the

earth was beginning to awake to spring after a long, cold winter. It seemed bitterly ironic that Leslie should have died now, just before nature's resurgence of life. She remembered how, when she was well enough, Leslie had loved to watch the slow progress of the bulbs forcing their way through the cold earth. It had been a winter of record frosts and snowfalls, and she had had to wait a long time to see the first snowdrops and crocuses bloom.

Someone touched her on her arm and she swung round. The Vicar was watching her compassionately.

In those last few months he had called regularly to see Leslie. Neither of them had any deep-founded religious beliefs, but she had been able to see how cheered Leslie was by his visits.

Now she was gone forever, buried deep in the earth of this North London cemetery.

'It's too cold to stand here. Would you like to come back to the Vicarage and have a cup of tea——'

There were no other mourners; Leslie had wanted it that way. She had no family, and the other people who could have been present would have been her friends and colleagues from the publishing world.

Diana started to refuse and then nodded. She didn't want to be alone. She didn't think she could face going back to their empty flat.

All the legal details had been seen to already. She had contacted Leslie's solicitor as her friend had asked her to do. She swallowed the painful lump in her throat. She already knew that her friend had made her her sole legatee. They had argued about it. Diana had suggested that Leslie should donate any money she had to medical research, but Leslie had shaken her head.

'No, I want you to have it,' she had insisted, and

because any form of argument, no matter how slight, had wasted her fragile strength deplorably, Diana had given in.

She had an appointment to see the solicitor, Mr Soames, later in the afternoon, but right now she didn't want to think about that. She didn't want to think about anything ... anything ...

She turned and followed the Vicar, pausing to look over her shoulder one last time, and say a painful final goodbye to her friend.

Leslie's solicitor, now *her* solicitor, Diana reminded herself, was a partner in a very old, established city firm who had been recommended to Leslie when her first manuscript was sold.

'Rather old-fashioned, with county connections,' was how Leslie had once described him to Diana. 'I get the impression that most of his clients are of the "gentlemen farmer" fraternity—good solid yeoman stock. Frightfully British, and very, very honest—that's Mr Soames.'

'Miss Johnson, please sit down ...'

Diana suspected that everything Leslie had told her about him was perfectly true, as she studied the plump, middle-aged lawyer, sitting opposite her. He was sensitive enough not to offer any formal condolences, for which she was very grateful.

His office was furnished just as an old-fashioned solicitor's office ought to be, with a traditional partners' desk, and a wall full of glass-fronted bookshelves holding fat and no doubt dusty tomes. Even the telephone was the old-fashioned, plain black traditional variety. Diana refused his offer of a cup of tea, and waited as he unfolded the document on his desk, discarding the pink tape which had tied it.

'I know you are already familiar with the contents of Miss Smith's Will. You are the sole legatee.' He mentioned a sum of money that made Diana gasp in shock. 'And then there is the flat you shared with her. You each owned half of it, but now, of course, you are the sole owner.'

He put down his papers and studied her over the top of his glasses. 'If you will take my advice, Miss Johnson, you will make use of this bequest to make a fresh start in life. This isn't the advice I normally give newly bereaved clients; the comfort of familiar things, familiar places, is something they need to cling to, but in your case . . .'

Diana stood up abruptly. She knew what Mr Soames meant, and part of her knew that he was right. Already she was dreading going back to the empty flat; not solely because Leslie was no longer there, but because its very atmosphere had become imbued with the hopeless misery of those last agonising weeks; and she could no longer bear to so much as walk inside it.

They shook hands and she left his office, stepping out into the harsh spring sunlight. On impulse she hailed a taxi and gave the name of a prestigious London hotel.

She would spend the night there. That would give her breathing-space. Leslie's doctor had given her a small prescription of sleeping pills which he had advised her to use if need be, but until now she had not bothered to resort to them. There had been too much to do . . . too much to keep her busy. Sorting out Leslie's clothes . . . things like that. But now she longed to sleep, and the blessed anonymity of a hotel bedroom was the ideal place for her right now.

The foyer of the hotel was busy. There was a

conference on, the clerk told her when Diana booked in. Perhaps because of this no one seemed to notice that she had no luggage, and she was speedily shown up to a very elegant bedroom, the last one they had empty, according to the clerk.

Once inside, she closed the curtains, and then opened her private mini-bar with the key provided.

The staff *were* busy, she reflected, as she noticed that someone had removed some of the stock from the bar, and that it had not been replaced. There was even a glass on the coffee-table. Ignoring it, Diana poured herself a generous gin and tonic, and took it through to the bathroom with her.

At another time she would have enjoyed sampling the wide range of exclusive toiletries provided, but now all she wanted to do was to soak in a long hot bath and then to go to sleep.

She took one of the tablets, grimacing wryly as she swallowed it down with a mouthful of her drink. Mixing drink and drugs—hardly a sensible thing to do, but she didn't feel like being sensible right now.

Diana lay in the bath until she felt the combination of alcohol and drug beginning to take effect, and then she clambered out and pulled on the terry-towelling robe provided, without bothering to dry herself.

The closed curtains gave the bedroom an eerie underwater effect heightened by the muted sunlight coming in through the windows. She lay down on the bed and closed her eyes, letting oblivion sweep over her, gradually carrying her out into its depths.

Marcus Simons grimaced as he glanced at his watch. The conference had dragged on longer than expected, and then he had had a meeting to go to that had extended into dinner. Now it was gone one o'clock, and he was ready to drop.

Whenever he came to London it affected him like this. Funny really—in the days when he had worked in the City he had found it invigorating and stimulating. Now all he wanted was to get back to the farm.

Ten years ago, when he had inherited the farm from his uncle, managing it himself had been the last thing he had intended. It had been the last thing that Sandra had intended as well. His mouth compressed grimly as his taxi deposited him outside his hotel. He tipped the driver generously enough to merit a smile and walked inside.

Sandra had wanted him to sell the farm, and when he had refused she had broken off their engagement. It had hurt at the time, but now he was worldly enough to realise that he had had a lucky escape. There had been more than one woman in his life since Sandra, but no serious relationships. His sister, Ann, was constantly chivvying him about it. She wanted him to settle down and get married, and was forever producing a stream of 'friends' to that end.

He strode across the foyer; a tall man with a shock of thick black hair, and piercingly direct grey eyes.

He didn't look like a farmer; his charcoal grey pin-striped suit had come from Savile Row, and he had about him that cool air of command that said unmistakably that he was successful in life.

He leaned across the desk and asked for his key. The girl who handed it to him eyed him enviously, studying the tanned planes of his face.

Now that was a man . . . He smiled at her, and she felt a

frisson of response shake her body. Wow ... he was really something.

It was that peculiar time of the evening, too late for any lingering diners, too early for the night-club set, and the large foyer of the hotel was almost deserted.

Marcus made his way to the cocktail bar, and then changed his mind about going in when he saw the woman strategically poised on the bar stool. She and the barman were the sole occupants of the room. She smiled at him and he looked away, suppressing a mingling feeling of pity and annoyance.

Did he look like the sort of man who paid for his sex? She was quite obviously a prostitute looking for business. As he turned to leave the bar he shrugged away his annoyance. Probably to her all potential customers looked the same, and it was juvenile of him to feel offended because she had thought he might be a possible client.

For some reason this brief trip to London to attend the Farming Management Conference had disturbed him. It brought back too many memories. London reminded him of the world he had shared with Sandra. He had been young then; young and in love.

Now he was well into his thirties, and cynical enough about both himself and the female sex to know that love had nothing to do with sexual enjoyment. It had been a long time since he had slept with a woman; too long perhaps, he thought grimly, remembering his instinctive masculine reaction to the perfumed femininity of his host's wife at dinner.

It had been a long, hard winter, and there had been no time for extra-curricular activities of any kind; but tonight, with an exotic feminine perfume tantalising his senses, his awareness of the delicious femininity of his host's wife, accentuated by the silky slither of her dress over her breasts and hips, he had suddenly felt an urgent need for the soft warmth of a woman in his bed.

But not a woman he had to pay, he thought disgustedly, as he pressed for the lift and then stepped into it. Ironically, he knew that there were any number of women among his friends and acquaintances who would be more than pleased to have sex with him. Unfortunately, they were not here in this hotel.

He had long ago made a rule not to involve himself sexually with the wives or girlfriends of his friends; and one of his longest-standing relationships had been with an attractive divorcee. But she had wanted a second marriage, and so they had amicably agreed to part. Sandra's greed had made him wary of any form of commitment; and the farm took so much of his time that there was precious little left to spend searching for a wife.

The lift stopped and he got out. Dim lighting illuminated the corridor. He walked along it, checking the door numbers until he found his own. He slid the key in the lock and waited until the panel lit up to show that the door was unlocked.

The sight of the shuttered curtains threw him for a moment. He couldn't remember closing them, but then he reflected that it had probably been done by the maids when they came to turn down the bed. He fumbled for the light switch and depressed it. Harsh yellow light flooded the room.

Someone was lying on his bed! His eyes narrowed as he studied the towelling-wrapped figure. All he could see was one set of pale pink polished toenails and a cloud of amber-coloured hair.

The figure on the bed stirred, and he waited with impassively folded arms, leaning back against the closed door.

Diana's throat was dreadfully dry, and her eyes hurt. She opened and then closed them again rapidly as the too bright light stunned her.

God, where was she? She felt totally disorientated. She moved, rolling over, and tried to pierce the drug-induced mists befuddling her.

She opened her eyes again, more slowly this time, and then they widened in shock, the mists dispersing rapidly as she saw the man watching her. Instantly she was pierced with fear. She scrambled to sit up, clutching the robe to her, as she looked frantically for the telephone. It was on the opposite side of the bed, and he was closer to it than she was.

Who on earth was he, and how had he got into her room? Was he some kind of maniac? He didn't look like it, logic pointed out to her.

Summoning her voice, she demanded huskily, 'Who ... who are you and what are you doing in my room?'

There was a moment's silence and then he said drily, 'Odd, but I thought that was my line.'

It took several minutes for the meaning of what he was saying to sink in, but once it had a surge of relief flooded over her.

He wasn't an intruder at all, but someone who had strayed into the wrong room by mistake. She smiled at him, completely unaware of the effect her golden-eyed sleepy warmth was having on him.

Whoever she was, she had style, Marcus thought grimly. This was no ordinary lady of the night, that was for sure. How had she got into his room? Perhaps she had some arrangement with one of the staff—it wasn't entirely unknown, or perhaps she had just got the wrong man ...

'This can't be your room,' Diana told him. 'I booked it myself this afternoon. Look.' She got off the bed, and picked up her handbag, showing him her registration card.

For a moment he was almost convinced, but then he remembered something. Walking over to the built-in cupboard, he opened one of them and showed her the clothes hanging up inside.

'If this is your room, how come you didn't notice my stuff hanging here when you unpacked?'

Too late, Diana recalled the used glass, and the opened mini-bar. She should have guessed then, but she had been too wrought up to do anything other than seek the oblivion of sleep just as soon as she could. Even now her head still felt woolly, and her thoughts were confused.

'By the way ... where is *your* stuff ...?'

'I didn't bring any luggage.' She could feel the colour rising up under her skin as he looked at her, his thoughts quite plain to read in his mocking grey eyes.

Dear God, he thought she was a prostitute!

'Look, it isn't what you think. I ... I ... booked in on impulse.' She turned her head away from his and said huskily, 'Today ... today I lost someone I loved very much. After ... after the funeral I couldn't go back to our flat, so I booked in here instead ...'

She was speaking the truth, he could see it in her face, hear it in her voice, and he was shocked by his own sudden surge of disappointment. For Christ's sake; had he *wanted* her to be available? She wasn't even his type. He liked small, curvaceous brunettes, not thin leggy creatures with clouds of amber hair and tiger eyes.

She had lost someone she loved, she had said. Her lover, no doubt. He was surprised by the fierce thrust of jealousy that pierced through him. It must be some sort of hang-up from what he had felt over dinner. It wasn't *her* he wanted, it was just a woman ... any woman, he told himself derisively.

'Look, lady,' he told her tersely. 'This is *my* room, and right now I want to go to bed.'

Diana stared at him, nonplussed, and then remembered the desk clerk telling her that she was lucky to get their last empty room.

'Look, you've obviously got a home you can go to,' Marcus pointed out. '*I* haven't—at least not locally, so why don't I call you a taxi ...?'

Spend the night alone in the flat? Diana shivered. No, she couldn't, not this night.

'No, please ... I ...'

Please. His eyes had darkened over her whimpered plea, and he was looking at her with an expression she had no difficulty in interpreting. He wanted her. This tall, dark-haired man, a complete stranger, wanted her.

This was the point where she normally turned on her heel, and ran. She was used to male desire, and at twenty-five had had more than her fair share of potential lovers, but after discovering how callous and cruel men could be, she had rebuffed them all, keeping them at a distance. So why was her body turning all soft and molten inside, simply because this man was mentally stripping the towelling robe from her body, and caressing it with his eyes? Why did she feel this almost savage urge to go to him and lose herself in the maelstrom of desire?

She felt an uncontrollable need to experience the resurgence of life that only sexual communion could bring, she *did* want it, she realised fatalistically, she wanted ... no, *needed* that communion, that renewal of life; she needed it if only to prove to herself that death can be conquered, that life does ultimately triumph.

In this stranger's arms, she could forget the trauma of these last weeks; she could celebrate the reality of life; she could renew herself and feel really alive again for the first time in months.

At any other time Diana would have been shocked by her own thoughts, but now they seemed natural and normal.

The way she was staring at him made him feel almost as though she was looking through him, Marcus thought. He looked at her mouth, her lips half parted and quivering slightly. The bathrobe concealed the shape of her body and he suddenly longed to wrench it from her and to take all the feminine sweetness of her in his arms.

He fought to control himself, his voice grating slightly as he warned her, 'Stay here and there's no way I'm going to be able to stop myself from taking you to bed with me—you know that, don't you?'

Diana hesitated briefly, knowing she was teetering on the edge of a chasm, but unable to do the sensible thing and pull herself back.

In a dream she heard herself saying huskily, 'Yes.' And then there was no going back. She took a step towards him, and heard him groan. Fired with a wild determination that pulsed through her, she unfastened the tie of her robe and let it slide from her body.

What was she doing? She had never acted like this in her life—she must be mad. But it was too late. She was in his arms, his hands shaping and moulding her flesh, his mouth hotly demanding as it fastened on hers.

He wrenched it away to mutter briefly, in her ear, 'I don't know who you are, or where the hell you've come from. What I'm doing now goes against every principle I've ever had but, God knows, I can't stop myself. I know I'm going to regret this like hell in the morning, but all that matters now is the way you're making me feel.'

He wasn't telling her anything she didn't feel herself. She couldn't explain to him what was driving her, what she was feeling; and why should she? They were strangers; they each had a need—after tonight they would never meet again.

He picked her up and carried her over to the bed, laying her down gently, his eyes never once leaving hers as he quickly stripped.

His body was well muscled, sleek and hard, dark hair shadowing down over his chest and his flat belly. Diana looked at him in awe and fierce pleasure. Her previous sexual experience had been limited to clumsy caresses shared with fellow university students; the sensual side of her nature had been slow to blossom; and then before it could flower it had been cruelly destroyed by Randolph Hewitt's cynical cruelty.

The shock of learning that he had simply been using her had withered away her youthful urge to share her heart and her body with anyone. There had been no one since Randolph, but that scarcely impinged on her consciousness now.

Now she felt, deep within her, nature's remorseless drive towards the re-creation of life. She knew even as she looked into Marcus's eyes that the need that drove her was in some way linked to Leslie's death and the long, achingly unhappy months that had led up to it.

She was like a moth shedding its chrysalis; a phoenix having been destroyed in the flames and now being renewed.

She needed this ... this sensation of flesh against flesh, this fierce clamouring of her blood. She needed this man, here and now, she admitted, as Marcus returned her look, studying the naked length of her, making her skin burn with febrile excitement as his glance lingered intimately, like a caress against her flesh.

'I must be mad doing this!'

His thoughts only echoed her own, but they didn't stop the intimate melding of their mouths, his, hot and demanding, hers, meltingly enticing.

He kissed her with a hunger she hadn't expected. Somehow she had imagined that for him sex must be a regular and frequent part of his life, but the touch of his mouth against her own, the fierceness of his hands against her skin told her that she was wrong.

Neither had she expected the sudden spiral of excitement and anticipation running over her nerve-endings as he kissed her. Her need to purge herself of the horror and pain of Leslie's death in the act of procreation was something she could accept and understand—just about—but the desire she felt for this particular man wasn't.

She pulled back, tensing slightly, and heard him

growl deep in his throat, 'No, damn you, you aren't changing your mind now. You've already made me want you too much.'

But despite his words, the silken glide of his hands over her ribcage and against her breasts was almost hesitant, as though he was waiting for her to tell him to stop. His thumb brushed against her nipple sending a savage surge of desire stabbing through her. She saw the gleam of triumph glittering in his eyes as he caught the betraying sound.

'You liked that?'

She shuddered finely as he repeated the caress and then bent his head to roughly brush the aroused areola with his tongue.

Flames—spears of sensation pierced her, making her cry out and cling despairingly to him, her nails etching sharp crescents in the flesh of his shoulders. His mouth absorbed the whole swollen bud, bathing it in moist heat, drowning her in awesome pleasure.

She cried out, her body arching like a bow. Tiny droplets of sweat dampened her skin and made it glisten beneath the soft illumination of the bedside lamp.

'Beautiful ... you're the most beautiful woman I've ever seen, do you know that?'

He was slurring his words faintly, like a man under the influence of drink or drugs, his breath quivering over her sensitised flesh as his lips continued to caress her breasts, tormenting them with brief kisses and tiny delicate bites, frustrating her growing desire to have her flesh taken deep inside the hot cavern of his mouth.

His touch was unleashing a wildness within her that she had never known existed. She wanted to scratch and bite, to cling and demand; she wanted ...

Her hands slid over his sweat-slick back; her fingers drawing his head down to her breasts, a sharp cry of pleasure breaking the thick silence as he correctly interpreted her silent demand.

When the pleasure he was giving her became almost too sharp to endure she bit frantically into his skin, and felt his body shudder in open response.

His hands shaped her waist and hips, and then moulded her against his aroused male form.

The heat of him was dangerously exciting, firing her own blood, making her ache for the culmination of her driven need. His hand touched her intimately, caressing and enticing her to abandon herself to him, his softly murmured words of praise singing in her ears.

Under his guidance she caressed him in turn, but both of them were too impatient to linger over the preliminaries, no matter how pleasurable. After all, they weren't lovers, content to simply adore one another's bodies, but two people driven by different emotions but similar needs, to find together an elemental completeness.

At the first surge of his body within her own Diana was filled with a wild exultation. She moved instinctively beneath him, hearing the savagery of his indrawn breath, and glorying in the fierceness of his possession.

She didn't experience any pain, contrary to everything she had ever anticipated; her virginity might never have existed, so joyfully did her body welcome his.

Together they strove to reach the shimmering pinnacle of human experience; together they shared the awesome reality of the apex of human desire, Marcus's deep-throated cry of release mingling with her own husky sob of delight.

It was over. Diana lay, trying to steady her breathing,

while the world righted itself around her. In the wake of physical satisfaction came exhaustion, so complete and so numbing that she was deeply asleep within seconds.

Marcus looked down at her broodingly. He had just experienced the most physically intense pleasure he had ever known with any woman, and she had fallen asleep!

Now for the first time, reality hit him. She had used him as a substitute for her dead lover. It was like being tipped into a pool of iced water. When he surfaced he felt totally disorientated. Man was the predator, the hunter, the user and abuser of the female sex, so why did he feel as though he was the one who had been used? Why did he have this disquieting fear that his life was never going to be the same again?

They had had sex, that was all. He didn't even know her name ... She had simply been a body—a very beautiful and sexy body—but a body nonetheless. He must be crazy to be lying here in this emotional stupor. He ought to be worrying about far more mundane things. He reached out, unable to stop himself from tucking a stray lock of amber hair behind her ear. In sleep she looked like a little girl.

She mumbled something and moved in her sleep. The sheet slipped and revealed one creamy, rose-tipped breast, still swollen and flushed from his caresses.

Suppressing a fierce shudder, Marcus covered her again, and then swung himself out of the bed. He never wore pyjamas, but there was a spare robe in the bathroom. He put it on, and then eyed the bedroom's one easy chair in grim determination.

He had behaved foolishly enough for one night—he would spend the rest of it alone in that chair, otherwise God alone knew what might happen. He had been stupid enough as it was—insanely so. He ought to have thrown her out when he had had the opportunity. Against his will he remembered the look of aching desolation he had glimpsed in her eyes earlier. It must be hell to lose someone you loved to death. Who could blame her for wanting to hang on to life in the most basic way possible?

Neither of them were to blame for what had happened; another time, and things would have been different. They had come together as strangers, he thought broodingly, and that was the way they must part—for both their sakes. He had enough problems on his plate with the farm, without involving himself with a woman who was grieving for another man.

He would be gone before she woke up. They would never meet again. He knew his decison was the right one, but some part of him was reluctant to let her go. Some part of him wanted to hold on to her and ...

And what?

And nothing, he told himself firmly.

CHAPTER TWO

'WELL, Diana, you know your own mind best, but I must admit that I'm surprised. You've always fitted in well here at Southern Television, and somehow I can't see you living in a small country village, running a bookshop.'

'I trained as a librarian before I came here, Don,' Diana reminded her boss, 'and my parents lived in the country.'

'Oh, I see.'

She was surprised to see that he looked a little nonplussed. 'You want to be closer to them, is that it?'

Diana shook her head. Her parents had emigrated to Australia six months ago to be close to her elder brother and his children, and her decision to sell the London flat and start a new life for herself in a small and fairly remote Herefordshire town had nothing to do with them.

'No, not really, I just thought it was time I had a change.' As she spoke, she glanced instinctively into the mirror on the opposite wall. Her stomach was still quite flat, her body as reed-slim as ever; no one looking at her could possibly guess that she was three months pregnant.

A guilty twinge flared through her, and she bit nervously at her bottom lip. By rights she ought to feel horrified at the thought of her impending motherhood, but she didn't—she couldn't. Ridiculously, she felt as though she had been given a most precious and wonderful gift.

To go to bed with a stranger, and then to conceive his child, was so removed from the way she lived her life that even now she could hardly believe it had actually happened.

Indeed, when she had woken up that morning in her hotel room and found all trace of the man and his possessions gone, her first thought was that it had been a dream; only there had been that tiny betraying stain on the sheet, and the invisible, but unmistakable knowledge that her body had changed; that *she* had changed.

It had never occurred to her that she might have conceived, and for a while she had put her nausea and tiredness down to the after-effects of Leslie's death. It had been Dr Copeland who had somewhat diffidently suggested there might be another cause.

Diana knew that the doctor had expected her to be disturbed and displeased by her pregnancy; after all, she was a single woman, a career woman living alone; but what she *had* felt had been a thrill of pleasure so great that nothing else had seemed important.

Oddly, until now she had never even contemplated the possibility of having children, had never considered what role, if any, they might play in her life; but now she was as fiercely protective of this new emergent life within her as though she had lived her life with no further end in view than this act of procreation.

Her decision to give up her job and start life completely afresh had been an easy one to reach. She could not bring up her child the way she would wish in London. Leslie's legacy made her independent; wealthy enough, in fact, not to need to work.

However, it was one thing to decide to have a completely fresh start, it was another to achieve it. On impulse she went to see Mr Soames to ask for his advice.

He listened to her whilst she explained what she wanted to do.

'Hmm. I would not advocate complete seclusion from the rest of the world,' he commented when she had finished. 'Perhaps a small business that you could run by yourself ...'

'I'm an archivist,' Diana interrupted him. 'I have no training for running a business.' But Mr Soames wasn't listening, he was looking at her with a thoughtful expression on his face.

'My dear Miss Johnson,' he exclaimed with a beam. 'I think I may have the ideal solution. Only very recently, a co-trustee came to see me on behalf of a mutual friend—now deceased, alas. I was brought up near Hereford, and have retained some ties there. My client owned a small bookshop in a Herefordshire market town.

'She died several months ago—both the property and the business are extremely run down—I am an executor of her estate, as indeed is the gentleman who came to see me.

'Since there is no one to inherit, it has been decided that the property will be put on the market. I must warn you, though, that since both the living and shop premises constitute a listed building, certain restrictions are imposed on their alterations and development.'

Diana listened to him in silence. A bookshop. It was something she had never thought of doing ... But she had the contacts ... and the knowledge ... and her years with the television company had given her a keen insight into marketing and selling techniques.

A tiny glimmer of excitement flickered to life inside her.

'Are you suggesting that I might buy the business and the building?' she asked Mr Soames.

'Heppleton Magna is an extremely pretty market town, on the River Wye. None of my family live there now, but I have fond memories of the place, and I still have several clients there. If you are interested I could arrange for you to see the premises.'

Diana thought quickly and made up her mind before her courage could desert her.

'I'd love to see it, Mr Soames.'

Before she left his office, she had arranged to visit the shop with him later in the week.

'I shall telephone you with the exact details. My co-executor is out of the country at the moment—on business, buying bulls I believe. He is a farmer, so I shall have to accompany you myself, if that's agreeable.'

Three days later they went, and Diana fell in love almost immediately with Heppleton Magna and its surrounds.

The town was more of a large village, with red brick Queen Anne buildings surrounding the town square, and narrow wobbly lanes leading off it, where Tudor houses with overhanging upper casements pressed closely together. The shop was down at the bottom of one of these lanes.

Inside, the rooms showed the signs of neglect that came from having an elderly, proud owner who, according to Mr Soames, had refused to allow her friends to help her.

'She was in hospital for the last few months of her life, but she still refused to hand over the keys to anyone.

'You can see the results,' he added with a faint sigh, pointing out damp patches where water had seeped through the leaking roof.

The kitchen and bathroom in the living quarters were apallingly basic, and the bookshop itself, so dark and dim that Diana was not surprised to see from the accounts that over the last few years its takings had dropped drastically.

Even so she had fallen in love with the place; in a strange way it seemed to reach out to embrace and welcome her.

They would be happy here, she and her child.

The house was in the middle of a block of three and it had a long back garden running down to the river. Beyond the river stretched endless fields; and she had already ascertained that there were plenty of schools and other facilities in the area. She and her child could settle down here and put out firm roots. She remembered with love and gratitude her own childhood in the Yorkshire Dales. Engrossed in her own thoughts, she scarcely heard what Mr Soames was saying to her. Not that it mattered a great deal. She had already made up her mind. Just as soon as it could be arranged she was going to move down here.

On the way back to London she found herself wishing that Leslie could have been here to share the excitement with her. Unhappiness shadowed her eyes momentarily; and then she reflected that had it not been for Leslie's death she would not be making these plans, because there would have been no child to plan for. This child was nature's way of compensating her for the friend she had lost. She felt no guilt or remorse about the way her baby had been conceived. She had shut the night and the man out of her mind. They had no place in this new life she was making for herself. They had met and parted as strangers. For the first and last time in her life she had acted out of character. Indeed, sometimes she wondered, rather fancifully, if a higher authority had perhaps directed her actions that night. Certainly it was not the sort of thing she had ever previously contemplated doing; nor would do again. And equally certain was the fact that she had had no deliberate intention of conceiving—but she had. She touched her stomach gently and turned to Mr Soames.

'You *will* get everything sorted out as quickly as possible, won't you?' she asked him.

'Well, if you're sure, my dear. I'll have to have the agreement of my co-trustee, of course. He should be back within the next few days. I'll get in touch with him just as soon as he is.'

Diana wasn't listening. The property would be hers; instinctively she knew it. It was just as meant to be as her conception had been . . .

The move to Heppleton Magna was accomplished smoothly and easily. In anticipation of the baby's birth and the life she would soon lead, Diana had traded in her small nippy runabout for a much sturdier and larger estate car.

The flat she and Leslie had shared had been sold, and with it the modern, designer furniture they had chosen together. All she had kept had been various photographs and keepsakes. She wanted her child to grow up knowing her friend.

She had already transported most of her clothes and bits and pieces down to Herefordshire, and she paused beneath the window of the flat to say a final goodbye to it, before getting into her car.

A shaft of sunlight caught the bright gold of the wedding ring she was wearing, and she touched it lightly, her mouth curling in a wryly amused smile.

Perhaps it was wrong of her to pretend she was a widow, but the country wasn't London, where single parents were almost the norm. Heppleton Magna had a predominantly elderly population, and she had no intention of allowing her child to grow up under the shadow of their disapproval.

Of course, there would come a time when he or she would ask about its father. Quite what she would say she had no idea. It would be difficult to make anyone understand the force that had driven her that night. She wasn't sure she understood it properly herself, and she was sometimes inclined to wonder if her behaviour hadn't at least in part been motivated by that extremely large gin and tonic she had consumed, on top of a sleeping pill.

It wasn't important now, now it had happened, she told herself firmly. She was on the brink of starting a new life; it was time to put the past well and truly behind her.

She didn't rush the journey—after all, there was plenty of time. She stopped off for a leisurely lunch and arrived at her new home late in the afternoon. A heavy workload at the TV station had meant that she had had no time to spare to furnish or equip her new home before leaving London so she had taken the precaution of booking herself into the local pub for a couple of weeks.

Because her new property was a listed building there were certain rules and regulations she would have to abide by in any alterations and improvements she had carried out, but luckily she had discovered a building firm locally who specialised in renovation and repairs of the kind she would need. She had an appointment to meet with their representative in the morning, when they would go over the house and shop together to list and discuss what had to be done.

She knew exactly how she wanted her home to look. The building was three storeys high, with a lovely large sitting-room, a breakfast-room/kitchen, and two good-sized bedrooms, so she would have plenty of space.

The almost euphoric sense of freedom and happiness that possessed her these days must be something to do with her changing hormone structure, she decided guiltily as she thought of Leslie. Her friend would have wanted her to be happy though, she knew that. The baby—her new life—these were fate's bonuses and she must look upon them as such.

The local pub was another Queen Anne building; next to it was the Rectory, and next to that the church and the small local school; all relics from the days when a rich landowner had designed that part of the town to please a new wife, who had been entranced with their quaint prettiness.

Diana had a room overlooking the rear of the pub. The river flowed past the bottom of the long garden—the same river that flowed past her own, and she made a mental note to ensure that at some stage she had adequate, childproof fencing erected as a protective measure.

The room's four-poster bed was part of the original furnishings of the pub; it was huge and cavernous, and Diana surveyed it with a certain amount of wry bemusement. This was a bed for lovers, for couples.

Off it was her bathroom and a small sitting-room. She could if she wished either have her meals in her suite, or take them downstairs in the dining-room.

After she had unpacked, she wasn't hungry enough to want to eat again, and so instead she decided to go for a quiet stroll around the town.

The town was still very much a working country town whose businesses focused on the needs of the local farming population. The Queen Anne 'village' had long ago become part of the growing market town, which was now a mish-mash of several architectural styles. In the centre was an attractive town square, and the cattle market. Her own property fronted on to this square, and was in the busier area of the town.

As she wandered around she discovered, tucked away down a narrow alley, an interesting looking dress shop. As yet her figure had barely changed, but new clothes of the fashionable variety would be something she wouldn't need to buy for some considerable time.

She paused to linger for a moment outside a shop selling nursery equipment and childrens' clothes. She could see from the window display that the shop catered for the wealthier inhabitants of the town. Of course, this part of the country was well established as a rich farming community.

A very traditional coach-built pram caught her eye and she found herself imagining what it would be like to push. A small fugitive smile tugged at her mouth. What was happening to her? She had never once in her life imagined herself having such maternal feelings and longings, and yet here she was drooling over prams. How Leslie would have laughed.

For the first time it struck her that she had no one

with whom she could share her pleasure in the coming child. Her parents and brother were too far away, and even if they had not been, she knew that they would have been shocked at her disregard of all the conventions. They would have loved and supported her of course, but ... but they wouldn't have understood.

She would make new friends, she told herself sturdily. She wouldn't always be a stranger here.

Her meeting with the builder proved more rewarding than she had dared to hope. Contrary to her expectations he was not full of doubts and criticisms of her plans, but enthusiastically entered into them. It was obvious from his conversation that he considered himself and the men who worked for him to be craftsmen, and he had a craftsman's pride in his work. He only struck one worrying note, and that was over the large beams upstairs which she wanted to expose.

'One or two of them will have to be replaced,' he told her forthrightly, 'and you'll only be able to do that with original beams of the same period.'

Diana felt her heart sink. She had planned her entire decorative scheme around a very traditional exposed beam and plaster background, and now he was virtually telling her that that was impossible.

'I think I know where you can get some,' he told her, lifting her spirits immediately. 'They've got some for sale at Whitegates Farm. They're from a barn that was struck by lightning and had to come down.'

Whitegates Farm—the name rang a bell, and then Diana remembered Mr Soames telling her that it was the home of his co-trustee.

'Will they sell them to me?' she asked uncertainly.

The builder smiled at her. 'I should think so. You'd

better telephone first to make an appointment though,' he warned her. 'This is a busy time for farmers. I'll negotiate the sale for you myself if you prefer it.'

In some ways she did, but she was going to be living in this new environment, and it was up to her to make contact with its inhabitants.

'I'll ring the farm as soon as I get back to the pub,' she promised him.

A woman answered the phone, but when Diana put her request to her she explained that she was only the housekeeper.

'You'll have to come out and talk to Mr Simons about that,' she told Diana. 'He'll be here in the morning if that's any use to you?'

Confirming the appointment, Diana got directions from her and then hung up.

The weather had turned pleasantly mild. She closed her eyes, seduced by the warmth of the sun coming in through the window. Next summer she could sit in her garden and watch her baby crawling on the lawn. She put her hand over her stomach and smiled to herself. The man who had fathered her child had melted into the mists of all those things she preferred not to think about. Before leaving London she had had a doctor's appointment, and they had frowned at the hospital over her lack of knowledge about her child's father. There were medical details they needed for the records, and Diana had been made to feel like a thoughtless and rather stupid child.

The stock owned by the previous owner had been packed away in several large cases, and Diana spent the afternoon checking through them. Apart from a few handfuls of books of curiosity value to collectors there was very little that was saleable. Some of the books had very nice leather bindings, though, and she resolved to keep them for display purposes on her own bookshelves.

Before leaving London she had visited various wholesalers to discuss the type of stock she wanted to carry. No firm orders could be given until the restoration and redecoration work was completed, but she had learned the value of good PR work whilst working for the television company, and on her list of things to do was a visit to the offices of the local newspaper, plus a tentative question mark against the idea of an opening party.

In the children's section of the shop she intended to have a mural painted, depicting a variety of fairy-tale and animal creatures. The same firm she and Leslie had employed to decorate their London flat would attend to that for her ... perhaps she would have a mural in the nursery as well.

She was doing it again, she derided herself, she was slipping away into her private day-dream, all too content to let the rest of the world slip by. Were all pregnant women like this? She tried to think of the ones she had known, all of them busy career women with homes and husbands to care for. How on earth had they coped with this almost total slowing down, this change to a life at a much different tempo?

With her pregnancy had come a sense of tranquillity quite unlike anything she had previously experienced. She could not even do more than mildly berate herself for the manner in which her child had been conceived; her rare flashes of guilt totally overwhelmed in the following rush of delight that flooded her every time she thought about the baby.

This would be her child, and hers alone, and she was quite happy that it should be that way. This new life had been started accidentally, and she could only look upon it as a God-given gift to show her that death, however painful, is merely another chapter of life, and not its end.

The morning sickness which had plagued her on and off since the start of her pregnancy returned with full force in the morning, and briefly she contemplated cancelling her appointment at Whitegates Farm. However, after a cup of tea and two dry biscuits, she began to feel a little better, and by ten o'clock she was quite looking forward to the drive out to the farm.

It was another warm day, with the sun shining and, knowing how hot it would be in the car, she dressed comfortably in a loose white cotton T-shirt top, and a gently gathered matching skirt.

Although to the discerning eye her pregnancy was beginning to be visible, and she herself could certainly see the changes in her body, she was still able to wear her normal clothes. Bright espadrilles, the same deep pink as her nail polish, adorned her feet, and matching sunglasses shaded her eyes.

It wasn't until the landlady gave her a rather startled second look that Diana realised how very different her clothes were from those worn by the locals. Working in TV she had naturally adopted the same attitude towards fashion and design as her colleagues, and she co-ordinated and chose her clothes with this in mind almost automatically.

On the way to her car she collected a few more appreciative glances, mostly male. It was rather flattering to be studied with such interest, in London her appearance would have merited no more than the briefest glance.

As she had known it would be, the car was like an oven with the sun beating through the glass, so she opened the windows and turned the fan on to 'cold'.

The directions she had been given were easy to follow, and soon she found herself driving along a road bordered by rich farmlands, both arable and pasture. Fields, heavy with crops, and criss-crossed by hedges, stretched away to the horizon, their colourscope of greens and golds occasionally broken up by a sprinkling of cattle.

The farm was larger than she had anticipated, a mingling of Tudor and Queen Anne, and very beautiful.

She had not expected the gardens that surrounded it either, and she realised the moment she turned into the open white gates and drove down the immaculate gravel driveway that this was more than merely a working farm. This was a showplace, she thought breathlessly, as she parked and admired the view in front of her.

The morning sunlight glittered on the mullioned windows set amongst dark beams and sparkling white plasterwork. It turned the red brick of the Queen Anne walls deeply rosy, and shimmered on the surface of the ornamental pond framed by willows and green lawns.

The drive had brought her to the front of the house, but now she could see that it continued around the side, and she frowned, wondering if perhaps she ought more properly to have driven round there. When she set out she had not envisaged that she might be coming to the sort of place where it mattered whether one chose the front or the back entrance.

Just as she was pondering her dilemma the front door opened and a tall stately woman in her late fifties came out, and called her name.

'I saw you drive up,' she said, when Diana stepped forward. 'I'm Mrs Jenkins, the housekeeper. I'm afraid Mr Simons is going to be delayed for ten minutes or so. If you'd like to come inside, I'll take you to his study.'

The elegant rectangular hallway was in the older part of the building, the stairs going up from it were dark oak and very warm. A richly patterned carpet in reds and blues emphasised the cream walls and dark woodwork. A refectory table in oak gleamed with polish, reflecting the copper bowl of roses standing on its surface.

'If you'll just come this way, miss.'

A traditional latched door led down a step to a flagged stone passage. Through a tiny window Diana caught a glimpse of buildings and a cobbled yard, and realised that the passage must lead to the back of the house.

At the end of the passage was another door. The housekeeper opened it and stood to one side to allow Diana to enter the room.

'This is the most beautiful place,' she murmured appreciatively, unable to hold back the comment.

'Yes, it is. This part of the house used to be the old still rooms. It was converted into office space in Mr Simons' uncle's time, but things have changed a lot since those days.'

Diana realised what she meant as she walked into the room and saw the array of modern technology arranged before her.

One entire wall of the room was filled with filing cabinets. On a very utilitarian desk stood a computer terminal with all the ancilliary equipment, plus a modern computer-linked telephone.

Like the passage, the floor was flagged, and struck

chill through the thin soles of her sandals. Central heating had obviously been installed at some time, and there was also a huge open fireplace. A modern filter coffee machine stood next to an electronic typewriter.

'The men are in and out of this room constantly, that's why Mr Simons uses it. It's convenient for them, and they don't have to worry about treading muck and dirt in. Farming isn't what it used to be. Would you like something to drink while you're waiting. Tea ... coffee?'

All her adult life Diana had been a coffee fiend; now all she could tolerate was tea—weak tea.

'Mr Simons won't be very long,' the housekeeper promised her as she withdrew.

Alone in the room, Diana was conscious of the thickness of the walls and the stillness of the air inside. She sat down on a leather chair and looked out of the window.

In the yard outside were several pieces of farm machinery. She saw a man trudge out of one of the barns; he was small and gnarled, and she watched his progress as he swung himself up into one of the tractors and then trundled off.

Obviously not the man she had come to see. The phone chirruped, and was answered somewhere else in the house. The housekeeper returned with her tea and a selection of what looked like home-made biscuits.

'Sorry about the delay,' she apologised, 'only Mrs Simons needed me.'

She must have frowned, Diana realised, because the housekeeper explained, 'Mrs Simons is confined to a wheelchair. She caught polio when she was twenty-seven.'

Poor woman, Diana thought compassionately. She knew for herself what pain could do to the human spirit; she had seen at first hand what it could do to a person to lose their mobility and independence. And for a farmer's wife, even an obviously wealthy farmer's wife ...

She thanked the housekeeper for the tea and sat down again. The cold was beginning to make her shiver. Her thin top and skirt, so suitable for the heat of the sun, were not suitable attire for this stone-flagged room.

She drank her tea, sipping it, and giving in to the temptation to eat one of the biscuits. They tasted as good as they looked. Once she was over her morning nausea, she was beginning to get so hungry; the weight she had lost during the long months of worrying about and nursing Leslie would soon be regained if she carried on like this. Not that she couldn't afford to put on half a stone or so, she reflected, remembering the doctor's warning to her that she must eat properly.

She was sitting staring out of the window, lost in her own thoughts when the door opened. She felt the draught of air, even before she heard the firm masculine footsteps and turned round.

The cup tilted crazily in her hand, the room blurring out of focus as the shock hit her. He stood in the doorway, frowning down at her, his recognition as complete and instantaneous as her own.

'You ...' Diana said at last. How, *how* had this happened? How on earth could this man standing here be that same man from the hotel bedroom in London? It was like the worst kind of nightmare; stretching the long arm of coincidence far too far. And he obviously thought so too.

'Well, well, congratulations on your detective work,'

he jeered, sarcastically, overcoming his shock faster than she had controlled her own. 'So you managed to track me down. I suppose I ought to have expected it.'

He was dressed in worn jeans and a plaid shirt, open to the waist to show the leanness of his chest. Tiny beads of sweat clung to his skin, and there was a streak of mud across his cheekbone. His hair was ruffled, his eyes bitingly dark, his stance that of a man who knows he's threatened but is determined not to give way.

Diana noticed all these things without really being aware of doing so, her mind only registering the meaning of his words minutes after she had heard them.

'What do you mean?' She stood up, trembling with shock and rage. How dared he appear like this, ruining all her plans, ruining all her happiness! She wanted to close her eyes and make him disappear. She couldn't believe he was real; she didn't *want* him to be real. She was ready to stamp her foot like a petulant child, only he wasn't going to go away. He was still standing in that doorway, watching her with brooding resentment, and he thought ...

He actually dared to think she had deliberately sought him out ... had actually and deliberately tracked him down! She froze with bitter resentment, and then another and even more appalling truth struck her. He was a married man, and she was carrying his child. No wonder he was so resentful of her appearance. A married man who cheated on his wife. Her mouth curled disdainfully as she controlled her shock.

'Mr Simons,' she said firmly, 'I think there's been some mistake.'

'You're damned right there has,' he agreed, cutting through the polite façade of her words. 'And *you're* the one who's made it. I don't know what you think you're doing following me down here, but you can just turn right round and go back where you came from.'

Oh yes, he would like that. Diana was seething. How dared he infer that she was chasing after him! Her eyes flashed warning signals, her lungs expanding as she fought for self-control.

'Unfortunately, you're wrong,' she told him crisply. '*This* is now my home.'

She saw the shock glitter in his eyes, and if she hadn't been so angry she might almost have felt hurt. After all, when they had made love he had been glad enough to have her in his arms ... more than glad. She clamped down fiercely on the memories.

'I've just bought a business down here,' her chin tilted aggressively, 'that's why I'm here, in fact. My builder told me that you have some beams for sale.'

'A business?' His frown had deepened. 'My God, don't tell me you're the one who's bought Alice Simms' shop?'

'As a matter of fact I am.'

She heard him groan and push strong fingers into his hair.

'I learned it was for sale through my solicitor, Mr ...'

'Soames,' he finished wearily for her. 'Christ, of all the coincidences. I don't think I believe this.'

'You know him?'

'Know him?' He laughed harshly. 'Didn't he tell you that I was his co-trustee in Alice's estate?'

For a moment Diana was completely dumbfounded. Of course Mr Soames had mentioned his co-trustee and she had even known that he lived here at Whitegates Farm, but the shock of coming face to face with the very last person on earth she had wanted to see had driven that knowledge out of her mind.

Her white face and strained eyes must have told their own story, because suddenly his attitude changed.

'Look, coming face to face like this has obviously been a shock—to both of us.' He reached out as though to take her arm, but Diana wrenched away from him furiously.

Oh, he wanted to placate her now that he realised he was in the wrong—and no wonder. No doubt he was terrified that she might spill the beans to his wife. God, what sort of man was he? She had never dreamed that he might be married. More fool her for not immediately guessing the truth.

'A minute ago you were convinced that I'd pursued you down here,' she reminded him bitterly.

'We have to talk . . .'

Oh yes, he wanted to talk to her now that he realised they were going to be neighbours, no doubt to ensure that she kept her mouth shut about their night together. He made her feel grubby and deceitful, she realised miserably. She hated the very thought of what had happened between them now that she knew he was committed to another woman.

'We have nothing to talk about,' she told him curtly. 'As far as I'm concerned we are two complete strangers, meeting now for the first time.'

There, that should make her position clear enough to him; that should soothe his fears. The thought that he had actually surmised that she had pursued him . . . that she might actually try to make trouble for him with his wife, regardless of the latter's feelings, sickened her.

He was looking at her in a way she found hard to

define; a mixture of rueful comprehension and masculine amusement.

Oh yes, now that he knew he had nothing to fear from her, he no doubt felt he was in a far more powerful and safe position. She hated the thought that they were conspirators in something she considered morally wrong. She had never been involved with a married man. She was fiercely glad now that she had adopted the mantle of widowhood. He would never know that she had conceived his child. Never.

He was shaking his head slightly, and grinning ruefully at her. 'I never imagined when I asked Derek Soames to sell Alice's place that this would happen.'

'No, I'm sure you didn't,' Diana agreed crisply, heading for the door. 'However, it has. Oh, and for the record, Mr Simons,' she told him from the open doorway, 'I do not run after *any* member of your sex, but most particularly those members of it who happen to be married. I hope I make myself clear.'

'As mud,' he told her with a frown. 'You and I need to talk.'

'No!'

She'd done all the talking she intended to do. For a moment, she thought he actually intended physically to prevent her from leaving, but at the last moment he seemed to change his mind, and he let her walk through the still open door.

More by good luck than anything else she found her way back to the front door. She was still shaking five minutes later when she drove her car out of the open gates.

At the first stopping place she parked the car and sat there, willing her lacerated nerves to heal.

Of all the most appalling coincidences. What trick of mischievous fate had brought them together like this? That Mr Soames—that most correct and proper of men—should be the innocent author of their dual misfortune, only increased her sense of disbelief. It was almost stretching coincidence too far. Almost as though fate had decided that what had happened was meant to be. Quickly she pushed the thought away, not liking its implications.

She gnawed desperately at her bottom lip, trying to quell her revulsion at his betrayal of his injured wife. *She* had at least been free to give her body to him.

But the consequences of that giving were something that had not even entered her head. She was carrying his child. She shuddered with pain.

If she could turn back the clock and change her mind about purchasing the shop she would have done, but it was too late. She had already put in too much time and money to pull out now. She was committed.

She herself had paid over the odds for the property because she had fallen in love with it and the town, and she had already admitted to herself that she would need the income from her legacy to buoy up the scant profits she would make from the book shop.

The business had been on the market for eighteen months before she had bought it; and if she tried to sell now ... No—she was trapped. The dreadful, clawing fear she should have felt on discovering that she was pregnant and had not, gripped her now. She could hardly wait to get back to the inn and shut herself in her suite.

It had never occurred to her to check where he had come from. She hadn't wanted to know.

In the shame-faced awakening to reality that morning all she had wanted to do was to forget the whole thing. She hadn't wanted to know anything at all about him.

They hadn't even so much as exchanged names.

Thank God she had taken the precaution of transforming herself into a widow, and she dimly remembered telling him that she had just lost someone she loved. If he should ever pose any questions she would have to claim that Leslie's death had been her husband's. Not that he was likely to question her, surely; he would be as anxious to forget what had happened between them as she was herself.

Her face burned hotly as she realised the connotations he had probably put on her unexpected appearance. He was obviously a wealthy man, no doubt he thought she was trying to blackmail him. No wonder he had looked so furious!

When the builder rang her later in the afternoon to ask about the beams she told him that she had changed her mind, and that she would prefer him to deal with the negotiations for her. He seemed to accept her decision without comment, but her heart was pounding when she replaced the receiver, and her hands were clammy.

The potential of the appalling coincidence that had brought her here to her one-time lover's home town were something she was only now beginning to fully comprehend. She had always made it a personal rule to stay clear of married men and she was filled with a sense of sick disgust for both herself and him.

To see him again in the flesh, in circumstances so far removed from those which had brought them together, had made her realise that in addition to drawing a convenient veil of forgetfulness over the entire night they had spent together, she had also painted a hazy, romantic mental picture of their coming together, subconsciously imbuing it with emotions and feelings that she was now forced to accept were totally fictitious.

She had deluded herself that something more than mere physical contact had existed between them, she admitted now. She tricked herself into the self deception that they had been lovers in more than just the physical sense, even if she was only now prepared to admit as much to herself.

She had quite erroneously and stupidly given the whole affair a magic and wonder that had lifted it out of the mundane and everyday, making it seem in retrospect something special, to be treasured. Now all her pretty pictures were being destroyed by reality, showing her that her child had not been conceived in a moment of mutual rapture shared between two strangers who in other circumstances might have gone on to be lovers in all the meanings of that word, but simply a sordid one-night stand between a married man, and a woman driven by excessive grief to forget all her own moral standards. It wasn't a pleasant thought. Her child's father was a married man with a totally dependent, sick wife.

She shivered suddenly. She must stop thinking about it. As far as the world was concerned, she was a widow who had conceived her husband's child shortly before his death, and it must continue to think that.

CHAPTER THREE

WHOEVER had first said that a lie once begun developed a life and pace of its own had known what they were talking about, Diana reflected wryly three days later.

Only that morning the Vicar had stopped her as she crossed the road in front of the church. He had introduced himself and welcomed her to the parish.

It had been obvious from his demeanour that he knew she was a widow, and Diana had hated herself for the lie she had been forced to give when he enquired if her widowhood was recent, but what alternative did she have? In a matter of weeks her pregnancy would be clearly discernible. When she had decided to move to a small rural town she had forgotten how gossip thrived in such confined conditions, and how openly curious people were about their neighbours' lives.

In London, she and Leslie hadn't even known the other occupants of their small block of flats; here, she was constantly being accosted by people who came up to her in the street and introduced themselves, exclaiming over the fact that she had bought the bookshop, and asking her about her plans. There was nothing malicious or unkind in their interest, she knew that, and if it wasn't for the unnerving presence of Marcus Simons so very close at hand, she doubted that she would have given it a second thought.

Somehow he had destroyed the cosy new image she had created for herself. It made her feel uncomfortable and guilty to be taking such pleasure in her pregnancy when his wife was an invalid. Did *they* have children?

The full enormity of what she was getting caught up in haunted her, but it was too late to make another fresh start.

Four days after her meeting with Marcus Simons, Diana received a telephone call from her builder, asking her to meet him at Whitegates Farm.

'I've negotiated the purchase of the beams you'll need from Marcus, but there's something else there I want you to look at. When they were dismantling the barn they discovered an old fireplace that must have been taken out of the Tudor wing of the farm at one time and put in the barn—probably to heat up animal feeds. You were talking about installing a traditional Tudor fireplace in your kitchen, and I think you should see this one. I've had a look at it, and it's a gem. The price is good as well.'

Diana would have given anything to tell him that she was quite prepared to rely on his judgment, but she could sense the excitement in his voice, and after her enthusiasm about the planned alterations it would look odd if she simply told him to go ahead without inspecting the fireplace for herself.

She had no need to worry, she told herself. He had obviously discussed it with Marcus Simons and he was hardly likely to be in evidence . . . far from it. She judged that he would be as eager to avoid her as she was to avoid him.

She couldn't spend the rest of her life avoiding the man; and she certainly didn't want to do anything that might give rise to gossip, even though common sense told her that it would be an extremely inventive, not to say intuitive, gossip who would make any connection between them.

Even to think in such terms made her feel guilty and grubby. She had always loathed anything underhand. If she had *known* that he was married . . . Realising that Bill Hobbs was patiently awaiting her decision, she promised that she would meet him at the farm after lunch.

The work on her new property was already forging ahead. Plywood panels had been removed to reveal a beautiful oak staircase, which was now being stripped of its ugly coat of paint and refurbished. She had chosen the reproduction Victorian sanitaryware which had seemed the most applicable to her plans for the house, but the work could not advance any further until the worn beams were replaced.

The whole house had been rewired; the underfloor work for the new plumbing was in hand. Things were progressing very well.

Two tough-looking teenage boys had come round and asked if she had any jobs they could do, and she had suggested that they might like to make a start on clearing the jungle that was her garden.

Amazingly, in view of their post-punk hair-dos, leathers and chains, they had proved remarkably knowledgeable, and she had been informed that her garden possessed a wide variety of fruit trees, plus raspberry canes and strawberry plants.

There was an old greenhouse down in one corner, with most of the panes missing, but they had assured her that the wood was sound, and had even offered to re-glaze it for her should she want them to.

She intended to ask Bill Hobbs if he thought the boys were up to the job. They had certainly worked wonders with the rest of the garden, and had proved surprisingly articulate whenever she had talked to them. But then, why shouldn't they? she asked herself, deriding herself for her burgeoning prejudice. Within a very few years she would be the mother of a teenager herself, and surely she hadn't forgotten the urgent need to shock and rebel that went hand in hand with those years?

Bill Hobbs was waiting for her when she drove up to the farm; this time she parked in the farmyard at the rear of the house. He opened the car door for her, giving her a welcoming smile. To her relief there was no sign of Marcus when she followed Bill into one of the barns.

The fireplace proved every bit as impressive as he had told her. She touched it with admiring fingers, shock jolting through her as she suddenly heard Marcus speaking behind her. She had her back to the door and hadn't heard him come in, but now her whole body was tensely aware of him, her hair prickling along her scalp.

'Bill, could you have a look at the window frames on the French windows before you go? I thought I noticed a touch of rot in them the other day ...'

He was sending Bill away. Diana could feel herself beginning to panic as the builder good-naturedly responded to his request and moved towards the door. She wanted to call out to him to stay with her, but that would only give rise to just the sort of comment she was desperate to avoid.

She made a move to follow him, her heart pumping frantically as Marcus stepped in front of her, blocking her path.

'What do you think of the fireplace, Mrs Johnson?' he asked her, his tone exactly the right one in which one stranger *would* address another. How many times *had* he betrayed his wife? Diana wondered sickly. How many times had he shared with other women what he had shared with her that night . . .?

He reached out and touched her arm, and she jumped nervously, her eyes going blind with shock.

Bill had gone and they were alone. She withdrew from him as though just being close to him burned.

'Why did you send Bill away?'

'Because I wanted to talk to you,' he told her calmly.

Diana turned away from him trying to force her lips to stop trembling. What was he going to do? Accuse her of following him again?

'There's nothing for us to talk about.'

'Yes, there is. I want to apologise for my rudeness the other day. Please put it down to shock. *You* were the last person I expected to see, and it rather threw me.'

There was no doubting the sincerity of his apology. It took Diana aback, making her lose her temporary advantage.

'I didn't expect to see *you* either,' was all she could say, her voice husky with shock and relief.

She moved restlessly, tensing as he reached out and touched hard brown fingers to her left hand.

'That night . . . you weren't wearing this.' He touched her wedding ring and she felt herself flushing with guilt.

'I . . .'

'You told me that you'd lost someone you loved. I didn't realise you meant a husband.'

'*I* didn't realise that you had a *wife*.'

She saw from his shocked expression that she had surprised him. He opened his mouth to say something to her and then stopped as a woman's voice called his name.

'In here, Ann,' he called back without taking his eyes off Diana.'

'My sister,' he explained tersely to Diana, turning his head briefly in the direction of the tall dark-haired woman who came in.

There was a definite resemblance between them. Ann Chalmers had her brother's grey eyes, and his bone structure, softened to suit her strikingly feminine gestures.

'Ma asked me to remind you that she's going out tonight, so dinner will be early. Oh, hello,' she held out her hand to Diana. 'I didn't notice you there in the shadows for a moment.'

Diana didn't miss the speculative glance she gave her brother, and her heart dropped like a stone. She was quite right if that brother/sister look was anything to go by; Marcus Simons did have more women in his life than his poor wife. She felt indignation burn inside her at the open raillery in Ann Chalmers' look.

'Ann, meet Diana ... Mrs Johnson,' he amended. 'She's bought old Mrs Simms' bookshop, isn't that right, Mrs Johnson?'

Diana confirmed that it was, and was then forced to deal with a barrage of questions from Ann Chalmers.

'And your husband, what——?'

'Mrs Johnson is a widow.' The harshness of the curt words seemed to startle his sister as much as they shocked her. There was a brief uncomfortable silence, and then to Diana's relief Bill Hobbs reappeared.

'Couldn't see any rot in those frames, Marcus,' he announced in some puzzlement.

'No? Oh, all right then, Bill. Perhaps I was being over anxious.' Marcus was so unconcerned that Diana knew immediately that there had been nothing wrong with the windows, and that he had simply used them as an excuse to get rid of Bill. But to what purpose? Originally she had thought he simply genuinely wanted to apologise, but now she was not so sure.

It didn't take an expert in male/female relationships to correctly interpret that look that had passed between brother and sister. It was plain to Diana that Ann knew that her brother was far from being faithful to his wife and that moreover she suspected him of having some sort of mild interest in herself. Now that he knew that she hadn't deliberately followed him, was he contemplating renewing their physical relationship?

Anger burned within her. If he did think that, he was going to have a rude shock coming. Did he really think she was the sort of woman who carelessly jumped into bed with other women's husbands?

It was only when she was driving back to the pub that the full irony of her thoughts struck her. How could he *know* what manner of woman she was? He knew nothing whatsoever about her, and that was the way she had wanted it to stay, only fate had intervened and confounded her plans.

It was only when she was sitting down in her small private sitting-room that it occurred to her to wonder what her reaction would have been if he hadn't been married. If he had been single and uninvolved with anyone else, how would she have felt? She bit her lip and gnawed worriedly at it, disliking the question and the thoughts it provoked.

It was only in the morning that she remembered that she had not asked Bill Hobbs about her two young workmen, and as arranged they presented themselves at the shop first thing in the morning, eager to know if she was going to employ them.

Bill was at the farm arranging for the transportation of the new beams and Diana frowned over her dilemma. Her own instinct was to let them go ahead. They seemed sensible and knowledgeable about what they were doing. Whilst she was wondering what to do one of the boys nudged the other and said, 'Look, John, there's your mother. She's coming over.'

Looking up Diana saw Ann Chalmers coming towards the shop, as patently surprised to see her son there as he was uncomfortable to see her.

'So this is where you are. I hope the pair of you aren't bothering Mrs Johnson?'

She spoke to her son, but looked at Diana, who quickly shook her head. 'Not at all. In fact they've been most helpful in clearing up the wilderness that was my garden.'

She saw Ann Chalmers' frown deepen slightly, and then her son said gruffly, 'Dad said if I wanted a new bike I'd have to buy it myself so Mike and I are just trying to earn some extra money.'

Her frown still lingered, and Diana intervened quickly. 'Honestly, they've been a great help, and I'm just about to commission them to replace the broken panes of glass in my greenhouse.'

It was obvious from Ann Chalmers' expression that she had no qualms about their ability to perform this task, and Diana immediately felt easier about her own decision. As the two boys left, intent on measuring up for the glass, Ann Chalmers said hurriedly, 'Look, I was coming over to apologise for my gaffe yesterday, I had no idea you were so newly widowed. Charles the Vicar, mentioned it last night. You must have thought it was dreadfully crass of me to be so obviously pairing you off with my brother. Luckily for me he's used to my attempts to get him married off. Hardened to them, one might say . . .' She caught Diana's quick exclamation of shock, and paused.

'Is something wrong?'

'Oh no, it's just that I thought Marcus ... your brother was married. The housekeeper mentioned a Mrs Simons.'

Ann's face cleared.

'She would have meant my mother. She lives with Marcus, because the farm has always been her home. In many ways it was a godsend when our uncle willed the farm to Marcus, although I must admit I half expected him to refuse to come home and take it over. I think it was the fact that it has been Ma's home ever since she was born that tipped the scales. So you thought Marcus was married,' she mused giving Diana a studied look. 'I can't wait to tell him that. He thinks that all married men have an unmistakable hang-dog aura about them.' She laughed heartily, unaware of Diana's chagrin. The last thing she wanted was for Marcus to know that she had been discussing his marital status with his sister, no matter how innocently.

The news that he wasn't married was something she found oddly disquieting. Why was that? She ought to have been pleased in view of her earlier shocked reaction to the distasteful information that she had made love with a married man.

Married or not, nothing could alter the transitory nature of their relationship, she reassured herself later when she was alone. Ever since she had realised that

Marcus and his family played quite a large part in the small community she had moved into, she had been frightened—frightened that somehow the future she had planned for herself and her child would be threatened by his presence. And yet why should it? Even if it should occur to Marcus that the child she was expecting might be his, he was scarcely likely to question her about it. No, if he did have any such suspicions he was far more likely to want to keep them to himself.

So why did she have this unnerving prickle of unease, this feeling that in moving to the place she had somehow put both herself and her unborn child in a vulnerable position?

Forget about Marcus Simons, she told herself that night as she prepared for bed, but in the morning she discovered that forgetting Marcus was something she was just not going to be allowed to do.

She was walking past the Rectory towards her new property when the Vicar emerged from the drive.

He greeted her with a smile and fell into step beside her.

'Ann Chalmers tells me that you are employing John and young Mike Henries to repair your greenhouse. I'd be interested in learning how they cope. I'm trying to establish a workforce of young people to do voluntary jobs for our elderly residents. It was Marcus's idea really, but I think it's a good one.'

Fortunately for her equilibrium, they had reached her shop, and Diana was able to excuse herself, having promised the Vicar to let him have a progress report on the boys' endeavours.

It was a pleasant surprise to walk into the building and discover that the job of replacing the worn beams was well in hand. Two men were busily engaged in making space in what was to be her kitchen, to take the fireplace she had bought from Whitegates farm.

Bill Hobbs came forward to greet her, grinning when he saw her amazement over the amount of work they had accomplished.

'It's coming along now, isn't it? Marcus called in this morning to check that we'd got the beams here all right. He was very interested when I told him what you planned to do. It seems he's been thinking of re-modelling the Tudor part of the farm for some time. It needs it, of course. It hasn't been touched since before his uncle's time. Of course, the old man just wasn't interested after his son and his wife were killed in that road accident. Same accident that killed Marcus's dad, that was. It happened just after Marcus went to America.

'I suppose we all knew then that he'd have to come back to take over the farm. There are some as say he didn't want to do it, but then there's his ma to consider.'

Conscious of the fact that she was listening to what was little more than gossip, Diana quickly changed the subject, asking Bill how long he thought it would be before the major construction work was out of the way. After a sharp look at her, he took her hint and dropped the subject of Marcus and his family. Talking about him when he wasn't there made Diana feel uncomfortable; as though she were guilty of spying on him and his family. She had no desire at all to know anything about him, she told herself later, as she walked slowly back to the pub.

It was a hot day, and before she got there her thin cotton shirt was sticking to her skin, making her slow her brisk pace, and wonder anew at the restrictions imposed on her by her impending motherhood.

Until Marcus had so shockingly reappeared in her life she had never felt better. Pregnancy had brought a soft glow to her skin, and a new tranquillity to her mind. Knowing that she was going to have a child had helped her to face up to Leslie's illness and death. It was as though the child was God's way of giving her back something to compensate for the friend she had lost.

Perhaps some people would find her thoughts both foolish and blasphemous, but she found them comforting. Her baby wouldn't be a replacement for Leslie; that wasn't what she wanted anyway, but it would be a confirmation that life does encompass more than pain and hardship.

It seemed that, having once successfully completely banished the father of her child from her mind, Diana was now to be punished by hearing his name from almost everyone she met. Somewhere she heard that he had worked on his uncle's farm as a boy, but that he had always been independent, and wanted to make his own way in life. Someone else told her that he had had a good job working on a bloodstock farm in America raising horses, but that he had had to give it up and come home when his uncle died because there was no one else to take over the farm and to look after his mother.

But what struck Diana most of all was the great respect and admiration that everyone seemed to have for him. Whitegates was the largest farm in the area, and the Simons family a respected one, but Marcus, it seemed, was far more approachable and available than his uncle, who apparently had been a rather remote, aloof man. From the Vicar, Diana learned that Marcus had a keen interest in helping his fellow men; that he was generous to them in need.

She had felt so safe knowing nothing about him, hadn't wanted to know anything about him, but that unwanted knowledge was being thrust upon her, and it frightened her without her being able to analyse why.

She saw him once or twice in town, and on both occasions she deliberately hurried in the opposite direction, without being able to give herself a satisfactory explanation for her actions.

Another week went by, and the work on her property progressed. The time was approaching when she would be able to start ordering her stock. A few days in London, attending to one or two financial matters, and visiting the wholesalers while her pregnancy was not too far advanced, seemed like a sensible idea. In consequence she advised Bill, and Mrs Davies—who ran the pub with her husband—that she would be away for three days.

She left her car at home, and decided to travel by train.

It was a shock to discover how much the noise and pace of London disturbed her. This was *her* city, her home, and yet after a few short weeks away she felt almost alien here. The air tasted of dirt and petrol, and she felt choked by it. Her eyes ached for the sight of fields and trees, and her feet throbbed from the hard heat of the pavements.

Luckily her business was accomplished more easily than she had anticipated. All her friends had been people who shared the same professional world, and after the onset of Leslie's last illness she had let them drift away. She knew more people now than she had known all the time she had lived in London, and apart from Marcus's unwanted reappearance in her life, she had no regrets at all about her decision to leave.

She had some papers to sign for Leslie's solicitor, and afterwards she went to visit the cemetery, carefully carrying the small pot-grown bush of rosemary she had brought with her.

She planted it carefully, brushing away the tears that stung her eyes. She was not overly religious and in many ways she found it hard to associate Leslie with this small plot of land among so many other plots, but there was still something immensely soothing about the physical task of digging in the earth and planting the herb. She touched its leaves and sighed.

While she was in his office, Diana had mentioned her coming child to the solicitor, and he had cautioned her to make proper provison for the baby's guardianship, in the event of anything untoward happening to her.

'God forbid that anything *should*, of course,' he had hastened to say. 'But one never knows, and as a single parent you will not have the comfort of knowing there is a partner to share the responsibility.'

His cautionary advice had raised all manner of questions she would need to answer, and these taxed her mind during the return journey to the exclusion of everything else.

Her parents were her next of kin of course, but they were in Australia and intended to remain there. What if she was killed in a car accident or . . .?

Her baby would have no one—no one at all. He or she would be completely alone in the world—apart from Marcus Simons. The thought slid into her mind as seductively as the serpent tempting Eve. Marcus was her baby's father. Marcus was a compassionate, caring man; a man who was held in high esteem by all who knew him. A man who took his responsibilities seriously.

Angrily she refused to dwell on the subject. Her baby was her own concern and no one else's. She didn't want to share it with anyone else. She wasn't going to die ... nothing was going to happen to her.

She got off the train in an emotionally rebellious mood, resenting the solicitor for disturbing her with his cautionary warnings.

The scents of newly mown lawns and fresh air mingled with those from the cattle market, strong and not as sweet perhaps, but a definite improvement on the hot petrol-laden air of London.

It had been market-day, and several traders were still busy clearing their stalls as she walked past.

The sound of a car horn behind her as she crossed the market square made her turn and look over her shoulder. She didn't recognise the gleaming Daimler saloon car, and frowned slightly as it drew level with her.

The window came down and Marcus's familiar voice called out, 'Want a lift? I'm going past the pub.'

'No, I don't.'

She knew that her refusal was curt and even aggressive, and she felt herself flush guiltily. One dark eyebrow rose, the cool grey eyes hardening just a fraction as he studied her.

She waited tensely for him to close the window and drive off, but instead he said softly, 'Get in, Diana, and we can argue about it on the way.'

She wanted to refuse; she intended to refuse, but she was conscious of being watched, and that made her feel more uneasy. This was a small town and people liked to gossip. The last thing she wanted was for her name to be connected with his, in any context at all—his, or any man's; so she stepped forward and climbed into the car.

'Madge tells me you've been up to London.'

Madge was Mrs Davies of the pub, and Diana felt a fresh stab of resentment. Why couldn't he leave her alone, why must he always be there? She wanted to forget him, to forget that one night of delight they had shared had ever existed. But it *had* existed, she acknowledged shakenly, as her eyes were drawn against her will to the hard length of his thigh as he changed gear and the car moved off down the road.

He was dressed formally, in a similar sort of suit to the one he had worn in London. Looking at him, no one would ever take him for a farmer; he looked far more like a successful business man—an empire builder—a traveller, rather than a man of the earth.

Only his hands, calloused and brown, betrayed the fact that he did not sit at an office desk all day.

She looked at them, and against her will remembered the sensation of them moving over her skin. Embarrassed colour crawled over her skin as she felt the intensive response of her body to those memories. She could feel her nipples hardening and thrusting against the confinement of her clothes. There was an ache low down inside her, a feeling of mingled anguish and need alien to anything she had previously known.

The road was deserted, and if he decided to stop the car now and take her in his arms . . . She felt the shudder of reaction grip and convulse her; it was like being torn apart by conflicting needs.

She wanted to escape from him, to forget that she had ever known him; to build for herself and her child a secure bubble which excluded the rest of the world, and yet she also suddenly, almost savagely, wanted to reach out and touch him, and more, she wanted him to touch her.

The car slowed down, and for one moment she thought that he was actually going to put her thoughts into words. She looked at him, her eyes wide with the shock of her feelings, the golden blaze dimmed by vulnerability. She heard him catch his breath, and then swear beneath it.

'Diana——' His voice sounded rough as though his throat was full of gravel. He reached out to touch her, and then she realised that he had only slowed down to turn into the pub car park.

Relief and embarrassment filled her to equal degrees. She was opening the car door and clambering out almost before he had brought it to a standstill, gabbling inane thanks, desperate to escape from the folly of what she had almost done.

'Diana . . .'

She heard him call her name, but she refused to stop and turn round. Her heart was pounding as she went inside, but he didn't follow her. Somehow she managed to answer Madge Davies' questions about her day, as she waited for her key, and then at last she was free to escape to the sanctuary of her own rooms.

Dear God, what had happened to her? She had looked at him and she had . . . What? Wanted him? She shook with reaction, almost collapsing on to her bed. Yes, she had wanted him; wanted and needed him.

It had just been some sort of emotional reaction to the solicitor's stern warnings, she reassured herself. She was bound to experience these odd emotional outbursts while she was pregnant. It was her hormones that were responsible, not her emotions! She felt nothing for Marcus Simons. How could she?

For some reason it seemed to amuse him to pretend that he wanted her, but he was an experienced man in his early thirties, there would have been many women in his life; the way he had made love to her had surely been proof of that, and Ann had more or less implied that her brother liked to play the romantic field, and that he had no intention of settling down.

He was, of course, a highly sexual man. Perhaps that was her answer. He had no regular woman friend at the moment; he was sexually frustrated and he simply wanted to renew the sexual relationship they had had in London. There was nothing threatening in that. After all, he wasn't to know that what for him was possibly a regular occurrence, had for her been a 'one and only'.

It was silly to feel threatened by him. Once he realised that she wasn't going to jump back into bed with him, he would stop pursuing her, she felt sure.

CHAPTER FOUR

ONLY he didn't. And worse, he seemed to possess something almost akin to second sight where her movements were concerned. It seemed that whenever she went to check up on the builders' progress, or bumped into someone in the street, Marcus was there as well. She told herself that she was getting paranoid, and that it was all simply coincidence, but when Bill Hobbs commented with a grin one morning when she went to inspect their work that he hadn't seen Marcus that day, she knew that she wasn't, and that other people were beginning to notice as well.

It was Ann, though, who confirmed her suspicions. Diana bumped into her one morning as she was coming out of the Post Office.

She had two of her four children with her; a pair of twin boys about ten years old, who looked disturbingly like their uncle.

'It's the Simons genes,' she told Diana with a grin when she saw her looking at them. 'They're disastrously strong. Michael, my husband, is slim and fair, and not one of my brood takes after him physically.'

Diana couldn't help wondering what her child would look like. She was due at the hospital for a check-up that afternoon and instinctively she touched her stomach with gently protective fingers. Because of all the weight she had lost when Leslie was ill, her pregnancy still barely showed. The fashion for drop-waisted dresses and voluminous clothes helped as well, but it wouldn't be much longer now before her condition started to show.

She could feel the tightening of her nerve-endings as she contemplated Marcus's reaction. She felt sick with fear at the thought of it already. He was an intelligent man ... he was bound to suspect ... to question her. But she would be ready for him. There was no way he was going to get the truth out of her.

'I hear my brother has a bad case of heart trouble,' Ann teased Diana forthrightly, adding with sisterly candour, 'Serve him right. I'm glad to see him on the receiving end of Cupid's dart for once.'

Diana couldn't pretend not to know what she meant. She could feel herself flushing.

'I'm sorry,' Ann offered contritely, pulling a wry face as she added, 'I seem to be constantly apologising to you for putting my foot in it, don't I?'

'Marcus and I are only acquaintances,' Diana told her. 'I hardly know him.'

'Not for want of trying on his part,' Ann shot back shrewdly. 'Even Ma's noticed. She asked me the other day if I knew what was making him so unlike his normal clear-headed self, and Bill Hobbs was telling me that he practically haunts your new place.'

'Oh, hardly, he's merely popped in once or twice to see how the work's going,' Diana felt moved to protest, not knowing really why she was defending Marcus. For some reason she didn't like the thought of him being exposed to sisterly teasing and ridicule, no matter how affectionately meant. Ann took her hint and changed tack.

'I'm glad I've caught up with you. I've been meaning to track you down and ask you to come and have lunch with us on Sunday. Oh, it isn't exclusively a family thing,' she hastened to assure her, as she saw her dubious expression. 'Michael is the local vet, and Sundays are often busy days for him, so to compensate for his absence, I tend to hold open house, with a buffet lunch, and friends dropping in, as and when they can … you know the sort of thing.'

With it put like that, Diana felt she could hardly refuse, and before Ann let her go she had extracted a promise from her that she would join them the following Sunday.

The restoration work on her property was well advanced now. The new beams were in place, and the ceilings and walls had been freshly plastered. Carpenters were busy at work installing bookshelves in the shop, and her kitchen and bathroom were taking shape nicely.

She had opted for a traditional kitchen with oak units and tiled tops. It was a well proportioned sunny room, overlooking the back garden, and with a flight of stairs that gave her direct access to the ground, thus avoiding having to go through the shop.

The internal stairs had been incorporated into her living-room. there was a small entrance hall with a cloakroom and a large built-in cupboard, and then on the second floor were the two bedroms and the bathroom. Eventually she could if she wished make some use of the loft space, and she was already contemplating opening it up in years to come to provide a play-room for her child.

She liked the town, and its people, despite their love of gossip. In her saner moments she felt that it would be impossible for anyone ever to guess that Marcus was her child's father. Everyone she met seemed quite happy to accept her as a widow, and when it eventually became impossible to conceal her pregnancy any longer she planned to say that the death of her husband and her subsequent discovery of her condition had made her anxious about losing his child, which was why she had kept the news to herself.

While she was in London she had managed to find the time to go into an exclusive baby shop in Knightsbridge, and had come away brimming with plans for her nursery.

Her home cried out for all the traditional prettiness of wooden cribs with pastel drapes, and she had managed to fit in a visit to the firm who had decorated the London flat, who had advised her to wait until the baby was several months old before adding a mural to the room.

Before she started worrying about furnishing a nursery, though, she needed to furnish the rest of the house. Now, with all the major reconstruction work out of the way, the interior was rapidly beginning to take shape, reminding her that it was time she started choosing things like carpets and curtains, not to mention buying herself a new bed.

The beamed and plastered walls made it impossible to think in terms of rag-rolled or wallpapered finishes; to do anything other than leave them in their natural state would be a crime.

The hospital she was attending was in Hereford, fifteen miles away, and after lunch she set off in that direction. It was her first visit to the hospital since leaving London but she found it easily enough, and parked the car.

There was the usual frustrating wait before she was seen by anyone, but after a cautionary word about her weight, a warning that she should try to put a little more on, she was free to leave.

It was almost four o'clock, and the pleasant warmth of the sunny day tempted her to stroll round the shops. An array of pastel-coloured samples of carpets in one window tempted her inside, and before she left she had made arrangements for someone to come out and measure up for her.

For practical as well as aesthetic reasons she had already decided to have the same carpet running through the entire house, apart from the ground floor shop area, and she had virtually decided on a soft mid-grey, which would allow her plenty of scope with a variety of colour schemes.

A deeply cushioned comfortable-looking settee, covered in a mixture of yellow, blue and grey floral chintz in another window, made her hesitate outside, and then on impulse walk in.

The information that their furniture was made to order, and their order list was over four months, was distinctly disheartening, but it appeared that the settee and another one like it had been ordered by a customer who had then changed her mind and, ignoring the feeling that she was being recklessly extravagant, Diana purchased them both. The covers were removable, and underneath the settees were covered in plain dark blue cotton, so they would be practical as well as attractive, and she would not need to be overly concerned about sticky little fingers touching them.

It was almost six o'clock before she left Hereford. The sky was overcast, and before she had gone more than a mile or so it started to rain.

She was five miles short of home when it happened.

One moment she was driving along quite happily, the next there was a muffled explosion and the car lurched warningly. She had had a puncture.

Diana drew up at the roadside and got out, inspecting the sagging tyre in despair. She had removed the spare and the tool kit when she was moving all her stuff down from London and she had forgotten to put them back.

She looked up and down the empty road, and back at the immobile car. From memory she suspected that there wasn't so much as a phone box between here and the outskirts of the town, which meant she had a long walk ahead of her in what was fast becoming a positive downpour.

She had no coat with her, of course, and her thin cotton shirt was already clinging clammily to her skin. The last thing she felt like doing was walking anywhere, but she had no alternative.

Getting back in the car she removed the ignition keys and slammed the door. Just as she started to move away she heard the sound of tyres hissing on wet tarmac.

Another car. She moved eagerly into the road and then stopped as she recognised the long steel-blue bonnet of Marcus's Daimler. Of all the people to be driving towards her, it would have to be him!

He stopped alongside her and opened his window, frowning as he took in her soaked state.

'What's wrong?'

'Flat tyre, and I don't have my spare with me.'

'Hmm ...' She was everlastingly grateful for his reticence on the subject of women and their folly. She didn't think she could have borne any male-orientated humour about taking the wheel out to make room for her shopping.

'I'll give you a lift, and we can stop at my garage on the way, and get them to come out and take it in for you.'

She would have given anything to be able to refuse his offer, but how could she? It would be madness to insist on walking into town in the state she was in now. She was already feeling cold and shivery; the temperature had dropped with the onset of the rain, and the last thing she wanted to do was to walk five miles, even to avoid Marcus Simons.

If she was less prosaically minded she might be inclined to think that fate was not so much taking a hand in her affairs, as poking in several exceedingly meddling fingers and giving them a good stir.

The inside of the Daimler was every bit as luxurious as its exterior promised. The rich scent of leather mingled with the cold rainy air she brought in with her, and there was something else, something comfortingly familiar.

It wasn't until she had settled herself comfortably in her seat and fastened her seat belt that she recognised it for what it was—Marcus's personal and cologne-tinged male scent.

She jolted upright, wincing as the constraining belt cut into her.

'Something wrong?' Marcus paused in the act of starting the engine to look at her.

'No ... I'm just chilly, that's all.' As though to confirm her words a tremor shivered through her, bringing up a rash of goosebumps on her arms.

She thought she saw a frown gather in his eyes before he turned away, and once again she marvelled at his fortitude in not giving in to what must be a temptation to remind her that she had no one to blame but herself. The thought made a small wry smile curl her mouth.

'What's so amusing, the fact that I have once again appeared in your life at an opportune moment? I suppose it does make one of us lucky, although I'm damn sure it isn't me.'

Diana stared at him. This was the first time he had said anything even mildly acidic to her for weeks, and she had forgotten her initial impression of him as a man who had his own decisive views on everything and didn't like them being challenged.

'As a matter of fact I was mentally praising your fortitude in not throwing in my face the fact that only a woman would be stupid enough to forget to carry a spare wheel.'

'Oh, you'd be surprised. I was once caught out the same way myself. Only I was a hundred miles from anywhere and driving a Cherokee. It's an American four-wheel drive vehicle, similar in principle to our Land Rover.'

Although Diana had heard snippets of information about him from a variety of sources relating to his time in America, it was the first time he himself had brought up the subject.

He looked at her now, his eyes narrowing slightly.

'No comment? I take it my beloved sister has been busily filling you in on my past history. Is that why I keep getting the cool brush-off?'

'No,' Diana told him bravely and honestly. 'Ann *has* mentioned you. She told me that you had a good job in America that you loved, but that you decided to come home when your uncle died.'

'I didn't have a lot of option really. Whitegates was my mother's home while she was a girl—she and my father were cousins; and then we all lived there when my uncle was alive. He inherited the farm, and my father was the local vet. If I hadn't come home when my uncle died it would have meant the farm being sold. It's been my mother's home all her life.'

Diana could tell from his voice that his hadn't been an easy decision to make. As though to confirm her private thoughts he added slowly, 'I've always loved horses. I did enjoy my work in America and, more than that, there was a girl there who I loved. The boss's daughter, as it so happened. She was the queen of the local society set. She didn't want to come over here and make a new life unless it was in London. She wanted me to sell up and stay over there; I could have invested my share of the farm with her father ... but I couldn't do that to my mother.'

'And ...'

He turned his head, and Diana received the full force of the cynicism in his eyes. Grey eyes met gold, and hers dropped as he said curtly, 'And so we split up. She's married now, I believe, with a couple of kids.'

'And you still love her?'

'No, I doubt if I ever did in any of the ways that matter, but it taught me a lesson I've been slow in forgetting. You still haven't answered my question,' he pressed. 'If it isn't my sister's ambition to get me married off that's bothering you; why the oh-so-cool rejection?'

'I'm not rejecting you.'

Thankfully, they had reached the town square, and soon she would be able to escape, but instead of slowing down and turning into the pub car park, Marcus drove on, through the town and out again in the opposite direction, towards the farm.

'Marcus!'

'You're soaking wet, I'm already late, and besides you still haven't given me a satisfactory answer to my question. It seems to me that the only way I'm likely to get one is to kidnap you.'

He didn't speak again until they reached the farm. Diana knew she ought to protest and demand that he turn the car round and take her back, but the chill had reached right through her thin clothes now and she was shivering.

They went in through the back door, into a large kitchen with an enormous Rayburn standing against one wall. The air was redolent with the mouth-watering odour of cooking food, and Diana felt her stomach churn with hunger-induced nausea. She had only had a snack for lunch, and now suddenly she was starving.

'Mrs Jenkins, will you show Mrs Johnson upstairs? She needs a hot bath, and something clean and dry to wear. You've got ten minutes before dinner,' he told Diana glancing at his watch, and then adding to the housekeeper, 'I'll go and see my mother now, Mrs J.'

It was useless to protest, Diana found herself being propelled into the hallway and upstairs.

'I think Miss Ann left a few things behind after she got married. They'll still be in her room. It's this way, Mrs Johnson.'

They were in the Queen Anne wing now, and the room the housekeeper showed her into looked out over the fields, and down towards the River Wye and the Welsh hills.

'The bathroom's across the corridor,' the housekeeper told her. 'Mr Marcus keeps saying he'll get individual bathrooms installed for these rooms. There's certainly space enough, but he never gets time to get anything organised. This place needs a mistress! Oh, I do my best, and so does poor Mrs Simons, but it isn't enough. The whole house needs redecorating.'

Diana could see what she meant, and she was already mentally stripping the faded floral paper from the walls and replacing it with a more modern and classical finish; perhaps a soft-spattered effect, or one of the new ranges of pretty florals with matching bedlinen.

The bathroom was huge, with an enormous old-fashioned bath, and plenty of deliciously hot water. She lay back in it, unable to avoid seeing the changes pregnancy was making to her body. Without her clothes the distortion of her shape was immediately noticeable, and she touched the firm swell of her stomach lovingly.

'It won't be too much longer now. Are you looking forward to meeting me as much as I am you?'

She flushed as she realised she had spoken the words out loud. She had developed this habit of talking to her baby only lately, and occasionally when she realised what she was doing she felt extremely foolish.

Mrs Jenkins had found her a pair of clean briefs, and some jeans and a sweater. All the garments were a little on the generous size, but they were an improvement on her own clammy things.

The bulkiness of the sweater hid the bulge of her stomach, and she rolled the jeans up to her calves to take up the excess fabric. There was nothing she could do about her hair, which was now curling wildly round her face.

Her handbag was in the bedroom, and she grimaced faintly as she looked at her shiny make-up-free face. She looked about sixteen. She pulled a face at herself, and picked up the damp towels, depositing them in the linen basket.

Just as she opened the door, Marcus appeared at the top of the stairs.

'You've made it with ten seconds to spare,' he told her.

She wanted to protest that there was no need for her to disturb their meal, that she could get a taxi back to town, but he was already going back downstairs, leaving her with no alternative but to follow him.

'Oh, by the way,' he stopped at the bottom and turned to look up at her, 'I've phoned the garage. They'll pick your car up, fix the tyre and get it back to you first thing in the morning.'

Swallowing the feeling that he had somehow invaded and taken over her whole life, Diana thanked him.

'Ma, I'd like you to meet Mrs Johnson—Diana,' Marcus introduced, taking her across the room until she was standing in front of the pretty grey-haired woman in the wheelchair.

'Diana has very kindly agreed to join us for dinner tonight.' Immediately the tired eyes brightened, and she smiled warmly at Diana.

'How lovely! That's one of the main things I miss about not being mobile—the fact that I can't get out and about to meet new people. Diana ... of course.' Her glance grew slightly speculative. 'You must be the girl Ann's been telling me about. You've taken over the bookshop, haven't you? Lovely—reading's one of my favourite pastimes, but it's been nearly impossible to get decent new titles locally. I normally have to wait until Ann or Marcus are going to Hereford or London.'

'Dinner's ready, Ma,' Marcus interrupted, and Diana

forced herself to swallow the small painful lump in her throat as she watched the older woman manoeuvre her chair up to the dining-table.

The room overlooked the back of the house and had lovely views, but sitting looking out at them could never compensate for the freedom to explore and enjoy them on foot. The limitations of physical handicaps were something that one was inclined to accept at face value, until brought face to face with the reality of them, Diana recognised, as she took the chair Marcus indicated.

Despite all her doubts, she enjoyed the meal, surprising herself by the amount she ate.

Jane Simons was an intelligent and witty woman, who made light of her disability and expected others to do the same. She seemed to have a lively interest in everything that went on around her, and was, as Diana soon discovered, quite heavily involved in local community affairs.

It must take a very strong and special personality to be able to cope so well with the loss of one's mobility and freedom, and something more than that to be able, as Jane Simons was, to make another person completely forget that she was actually restricted to her wheelchair, which was what Diana found happening to her by the time the meal was over.

Marcus remained slightly in the background, throwing in the odd comment now and again, but at other times apparently content to let the conversation flow around him. Unlike Ann, Jane Simons made no comment on her son's single state, but she was not one of that breed of possessive demanding women who could not bear the thought of their son being committed to anyone other than themselves, Diana could see that.

It was just gone nine o'clock when they rose from the table, and Diana was surprised to realise how long they had been talking.

'I must get back.' She looked at Marcus. 'If I could use your phone to ring for a taxi ...'

He frowned. 'There's no need. I'll take you home.'

What could she say? To refuse would look both churlish and ridiculous, but once again the unease that had remained dormant during the meal surfaced.

Why couldn't he accept that she didn't want any further involvement with him, and why, more to the point, did he want an involvement with her? Because she would be a convenient bed partner?

They were half-way back when Marcus abruptly stopped the car and turned to face her.

'Now,' he said coolly, 'we can talk without being interrupted. Why is it I get the feeling that I'm someone you'd rather not know, Diana?'

'Why should I *want* to?' she countered unsteadily. 'When I first moved here you accused *me* of running after *you*. You didn't want to know me then, Marcus.'

'I was in shock,' he told her wryly, 'I'm not used to my dreams manifesting themselves in my office.'

He was smiling at her in a way that made her heart miss a beat. A tingling excitement shivered through her. This had to stop right now; she wasn't in a position to allow herself to become attracted to this man. And she *was* attracted to him, she admitted to herself, frightened by the realisation.

'I know you've only recently been widowed,' he confounded her by adding, 'but——'

'But just because I went to bed with you once, you expect me to repeat my mistake?' Her voice sounded shrill and unfamiliar, she was close to the edge of total panic. For some reason, hearing Marcus describe her as a widow increased her feeling of guilt. She hated lying like this, but he was forcing her to do so. It was *his* fault that she was caught in this morass of lies and evasions. If he had simply left her alone . . . She lashed herself up into a state of righteous anger against him, knowing that it was her own defence against the weakening tide of emotion she could feel growing inside her.

'Your *mistake*? Is that what it was? It didn't seem like it at the time!' The humour and tenderness was gone from his face now, leaving it hard and angry. 'You'd like to pretend that night never happened, wouldn't you Diana? But you can't.'

Without another word he re-started the car and drove her home. She was still trembling when she got out of the car, moving hurriedly and awkwardly before he could leave his seat to assist her.

'I respect your grief for your husband, Diana, but . . .'

'*Please*! I don't want to talk about it. Can't you see I came here in the first place to escape from the past? I wanted a new start . . .'

'And I went and spoiled it all, didn't I?'

His eyes registered her betraying use of the word escape, but he didn't say anything. He dared not—he was held too dangerously tightly in the coils of a frustration that was as much emotional as it was physical to risk pushing her any further tonight. He wanted to . . . He wanted nothing quite as much as to take her in his arms and make her admit that there was something between them, but he sensed that to do so would only add to her panic and withdrawal.

It *had* been a shock, seeing her like that, so unexpectedly in his office and for a moment he had thought . . . but it had been for a moment only; before he remembered how often he had thought about her since meeting her, and how many times he had woken up in the night, still half asleep, searching for the warmth of her body next to his own, only to realise she wasn't there.

He watched her go in frustrated silence. She was deliberately erecting barriers against him. He could almost feel them. Why? Because she felt guilty about making love with him so soon after her husband's death, that was why; any idiot could see that. He had to convince her that she had nothing to feel guilty for, but how?

Frowning, he drove home. It was odd, but he distinctly remembered the tight, almost virginal feel of her body when they had made love. He had registered it only fleetingly at the time, too aroused by the desire he felt for her to dwell on it; but he had had the unmistakable impression that it had been a long time since she had last made love; and had he been asked to do so, he would have automatically put the date of the commencement of her widowhood some years in the past. Of course, it could be that her husband had been too ill to make love to her; and that she, out of loyalty and love for him, had refused to take a lover. That would explain the almost frantic way in which she had responded to him; as though having him inside her was something she was prepared to die for.

Damn! He swore suddenly as he was forced to brake to avoid an obstruction in the road. If he didn't stop thinking about her, and start concentrating on what he was doing, *he* wasn't going to live to so much as see her again, never mind persuade her to let him into her life.

And he *would* persuade her. He was quite determined on that point.

CHAPTER FIVE

VERY gradually, Diana found that she was being integrated into the life of the town.

After living in London for so long, she still found it strange to be addressed by people she hardly knew with a friendly 'good morning', but now their faces were slowly becoming familiar, and she found that she was slowly leaving behind the acute bitterness and anguish of Leslie's death. It would always hurt that her friend had died so young, and surely so unfairly, but now her pain was beginning to soften and become more tolerable.

On the morning that Bill Hobbs told her that the property was now ready for her to move into, she could hardly contain her excitement. Long after the workmen had packed up and gone she wandered round the empty rooms, breathing in a mixture of wood shavings and plaster dust, uncaring of what the dust was doing to her clothes, or the emptiness of the rooms.

This was her kingdom ... hers and hers alone. She hugged the knowledge to herself, clasping her arms around her body. It gave her a warm, secure feeling, which she was intelligent enough to realise sprang originally from the awful fear and desolation she had felt on Leslie's death.

Because she could no longer trust other human beings to be a permanent part of her life, she was using the house as a substitute. Death could not take the house away from her. It was hers for as long as she wanted it to be.

Suddenly within her she felt a tiny fluttering movement, so brief and delicate that she held her breath, fearing that she was imagining it. That she should feel her baby move just at this particular moment seemed to be a good omen for the future. Ridiculously she felt tears prick her eyes.

She had things to do, she reminded herself. She should be working and not wandering around up here mooning. She had already decided that she would stay on at the pub whilst the decorators worked on the building, and when she rang up to tell them that they could now start work, she was congratulated on her foresight.

'We'll be able to get the work done much faster with the house being empty,' the decorator told her, adding reassuringly, 'My lot will be down first thing in the morning, and hopefully it shouldn't take too long. I've got all the details of what you want.'

Downstairs, in the shop area, the aroma of new wood was strongly pungent. Her pregnancy seemed to have increased her sense of smell, and she sniffed the air appreciatively.

The boys had made an excellent job of clearing the worst of the overgrowth from the garden. She hadn't decided yet what she was going to do with it. She would have to have some sort of fence erected along the river bank to protect the baby.

She went outside and wandered along the crazy-paving path the boys had discovered beneath the weeds and overgrown grass.

There was an ancient apple tree in the middle of the

lawn, and she was contemplating having a wooden seat constructed around it. It would make a pleasantly shady spot for sitting in. The vegetable plot was separated from the rest of the garden by a ramshackle trellis, which would have to be replaced. She would grow some sort of climber along it—not roses with their sharp thorns, but clematis perhaps, the old fashioned multi-flowered kind, and perhaps even sweet peas. Her father used to grow them at home in their small suburban garden and she remembered how she had loved them.

Some of the glass had been replaced in the greenhouse and she walked towards it. An old gnarled grape vine twined round some of the metal struts. It needed pruning; she would have to ask around and find out if there was someone who could come in and do the gardening for her.

A piece of roofing glass that the boys hadn't been able to remove caught her eye. She reached up to touch it, only realising how dangerously precarious it was as it wobbled and started to slide towards her.

Fear held her immobile, and she watched the glass fall towards her in horrified fascination until suddenly she was plucked away from the source of danger. She heard the tinkling sound of the glass as it smashed into the sun-baked ground but it was muffled by the protective pressure of the arms locked round her.

'Are you all right?' The harsh sound of his voice reverberated through her body.

Where on earth had Marcus sprung from? She hadn't heard him at all. Shaken by her experience, she felt a wave of faintness rush over her. Even as she fought against it, she heard herself give a tiny moan and felt the pressure of Marcus's arms tighten.

'Diana, it's all right ... you're perfectly safe.'

His voice was rough with concern, his body supporting hers, shielding it from all danger. She had a dangerously weak impulse simply to lie there and close her eyes enjoying the warmth and comfort of being held by him, but she thrust the weakness aside.

For a moment, as she struggled to be free, she thought he wasn't going to let her go, but then he did so. As she stepped back from him Diana caught sight of his grimly white face and realised how great her danger had been.

She couldn't help but look over her shoulder to where the sheet of heavy glass lay splintered on the ground.

'Those young idiots ought to be thrashed for leaving the greenhouse in such a dangerous state.'

'You certainly arrived just in the nick of time.'

'I saw the sun glint on the glass as it started to slide,' he told her grimly. 'I don't think I've ever run so fast in my whole life. Are you sure you're all right?' He reached out to brush some dead leaves from the grape-vine from her hair, and as he did so his attention was caught by the slight but unmistakable swell of her body.

He felt his breath catch in his throat, everything around him slowing down as his heartbeat speeded up.

'You're pregnant!'

It had arrived; the moment that she had been dreading, Diana realised. She wanted to turn and run from him, to hide herself from the devastating message she could read in his eyes as they moved from her stomach to her face.

'My child ... you're carrying my child!'

His voice was hoarse with shock—and something else—it made her panic. She had expected him to question her, but she had not anticipated this degree of certainty, this compelling assumption that her child was *his*.

Her mouth had gone dry with fear and apprehension. Alarm shivered down her spine, raising the tiny hairs on her body. Even her fingertips tingled with it.

'No . . .' Her voice croaked out from between her dry lips. 'No Marcus . . . it isn't yours . . .'

He focused on her, but seemed unable to see her properly. He looked dazed, shocked, and yet in some way pleased, and Diana knew that her denial hadn't registered.

It frightened her, this feeling coming from him that although he was shocked by his discovery, he was also pleased by it.

'It isn't yours, Marcus,' she told him again, her voice stronger this time.

Now he looked at her, his eyes darkening to the colour of wet slate, his mouth a hard line of displeasure.

'What the hell do you mean?'

'Exactly what I said. This baby . . .' she touched her stomach lightly, 'is my husband's. This baby is Leslie's.' The moment she said it she felt as though it were true, as though in some way she was having this baby for her friend, the friend whose identity she had deliberately falsified.

But she had had no choice, she pleaded with herself in mitigation. She couldn't allow Marcus to believe that the baby was his—she couldn't.

'You're lying!'

Despite the forceful tone of his voice, Diana had seen the flicker of uncertainty in his eyes. He was over the shock now, but she could almost see the thoughts

teeming through his brain. She would have to be careful
... so careful.

'No, Marcus, I'm not lying. I admit that when I ...
when I went to bed with you I didn't know I was
pregnant. The baby must have been conceived just ...
just before ... just before Leslie died.' Somehow she
managed to swallow down the bile of wretchedness
gathering in her throat.

'The last attempt of a dying man to preserve part of
himself for posterity.' He frowned suddenly, his face
harshly white and drawn in the bright sunlight. 'You
must have come straight from his bed to mine, and yet I
could have sworn when we made love that you hadn't
had a man in one hell of a long time. He might have
given you a child, Diana, but he didn't satisfy you,' he
told her cruelly.

She had to stop this. She had to stop him now before
he forced her to blurt out the truth.

'You're wrong, Marcus,' she told him huskily. 'He
satisfied me in the most intense way it is possible for a
man to satisfy a woman. He gave me his child.'

She didn't know where the words had come from, or
how she had come by the knowledge that they would
hurt the man listening to them; she just knew that they
would.

She felt sick inside as she watched him turn away from
her. A muscle twitched in his jaw, and she had an insane
impulse to reach out and touch him, to comfort him in
his pain.

He really did care she realised humbly, but he would
learn—as she had had to learn—that it was dangerous to
allow oneself to care. In the end he would thank her for
this.

Just as their child would thank her? She felt the pain of the thought burning through her. What she was doing was wrong! She was denying her child a right to know its father.

'Diana.'

'I think I'll go back to the house, Marcus. I'm feeling rather tired.'

'So cool and remote,' he taunted her, battling against his frustrated anger. 'But you weren't so cool in my arms, were you, my chaste Diana?'

Diana knew that he was deliberately trying to goad her and why, but that didn't stop the warm colour heating her skin.

'That was different. It was just the emotion of the moment.'

'And now you feel nothing for me at all, is that it?' he demanded bitterly.

'Nothing.' She forced herself to say it, and to look away from him as though the denial was true.

She knew he was angry, but she was totally unprepared for the way he seized hold of her, spinning her round in his arms, before locking her against his body in a way that made her feel intensely conscious of the maleness of it. Again within her stomach she felt that faint flutter of new life; almost as though their child sought to make contact with its father.

'So you feel nothing for me do you?'

The hardness of his mouth as it came down on hers bruised her lips, his hands digging into soft flesh as he held her to him, his tongue relentless in its heated exploration.

She tried to blot out what was happening but, as though some alien part of her rebelled against her will, she found herself responding to the savage passion of his embrace.

It was almost as though some part of her had longed and ached for this physical communion; as though some reckless part of her needed this fierce meshing of mouths and bodies.

She could feel the dark tide of pleasure surging through her, heating her blood and making her yearn for more than the possession of his mouth on hers.

She tried to tell herself that it was simply her hormones, that she felt nothing real or emotional for him, but her hands had crept up round his neck, and her breasts throbbed tormentingly as though her very flesh remembered and wanted the sensation of his against it.

She didn't know how long they stood there locked in a deeply sensual embrace; she only knew that it was Marcus who stepped back first, his chest heaving with a mixture of arousal and anger.

'You're a coward, Diana,' he told her thickly. 'You haven't got the guts to admit that you want me as much as I want you, perhaps you're *not* the woman I thought you were at all.' He walked away from her, turning only when he was several yards away to say curtly, 'If you want me, you know where you can find me.'

And then he was gone, leaving her feeling more bereft than she had ever felt at any other time in her life, including when Leslie died.

It shocked her that she could feel this intensity of emotion for a man she barely knew. A man who was the father of her child, she reminded herself achingly. She wanted to call him back, to run after him, and plead with him to understand. But to understand what? That she was too scared of losing him to commit herself to him?

That she wanted his respect and his friendship but that she couldn't admit the truth about her child to him? No, it was better that they part completely. In the long run it would be easier to deal with.

Shivering with a mixture of reaction and misery, she made her way back to the house. Suddenly all her pleasure in it had been dimmed. She wasn't looking forward to living there alone any more. All she could think about was the way her body ached in the aftermath of Marcus's savage kiss . . . about her child, and how he or she would feel about not having a father.

Why in God's name had fate elected to bring her here to this town, of all places? Why, oh why couldn't she and Marcus simply have been ships that passed in the night?

She could always move. But she didn't want to; she had lost that impetus that had driven her from London and everything she knew. She felt secure here, oddly so, perhaps in view of her almost daily dread of Marcus discovering the truth, but the worst was over now. He knew about her pregnancy, and he had accepted the story she had told him.

She looked down at herself; it was beginning to show. Now was the time to make her condition public. As a young widow, she would be expected to be delighted at the thought of carrying her husband's child. She could account for her earlier silence on the subject by explaining that she had been frightened of losing the child, as indeed she had, but those critical early months were safely over now. Yes, perhaps it was time for her to publicise the fact that she would soon be a mother.

Her opportunity to do so came sooner than she had expected. The emotional trauma of the morning had left her drained and tired, so in the afternoon she went into the pub garden, and relaxed in a comfortable cane chair.

Ann saw her there as she walked along the river path, heading for the vicarage.

'It's all right for some,' she teased. 'I thought you had a brand new house to decorate and furnish?'

'Don't blame it on me,' Diana called back, patting her stomach meaningfully. 'It's not entirely my fault.'

She saw instantly that Ann had understood her.

'When?' she asked delightedly, coming into the garden.

'Another five months. I've kept it in the dark up until now, because well . . .' she shrugged. 'After losing Leslie . . .'

'Yes, of course. You must be thrilled, though.'

'Yes, I am,' Diana agreed truthfully. 'Even if he or she is making me lazy.'

'Oh, it gets worse and not better,' Ann told her ruefully, 'but make the most of it. Once Junior arrives you won't have time for feeling lazy. By the way, I'm here to apologise on behalf of my eldest. Marcus really tore a strip off him this morning. I had no idea they'd left your greenhouse in a dangerous state.'

'I had no idea it was in such a dangerous state in the first place,' Diana reassured her. 'Otherwise I'd never have let them touch it. It makes me feel cold all over just thinking about what might have happened.'

'Well, you're taking it very calmly—unlike Marcus. I can't remember ever seeing him so worked up. He's normally very even-tempered. I've been meaning to ask you round for dinner one evening. Would Saturday night suit you?'

Diana wanted to refuse, sensing there was more to

Ann's invitation than met the eye. She suspected Marcus's sister was indulging in more of her matchmaking, but how could she refuse without giving offence?

'The Vicar and his wife will be there. I suspect they want to persuade you to join the Youth Committee; they're always looking for more volunteers for various projects.'

Ann was making it impossible for her to refuse without appearing churlish, and Diana suspected that she was well aware of it, despite her guileless expression.

'In that case ... I accept,' she replied wryly. She wasn't going to ask if Marcus would also be there. She suspected that she already knew the answer.

They chatted for a few more minutes before Ann excused herself. She was due at the Vicarage to discuss their plans for the summer fête.

'Marcus normally allows us to hold it in the paddock by the house. This year we're planning to be rather adventurous and hold a dance afterwards, but we'll need to organise an extra large marquee. If you can spare the time and you've got any organisational abilities at all, you'd be a godsend on the committee. Are you interested?'

She really ought to refuse, but she was good at organising, and surely that was one of the reasons she had come to a small country town, because she wanted to be involved in the activities. It would be six weeks or so before the shop could open. She would have the time.

'If you think I could be any help, I'd certainly be willing to give it a try.'

'Marvellous—why don't you come with me now? Kath will be thrilled; organising these things normally falls on her lap, and she's so busy as it is. You'd never believe how busy a Vicar's wife can be. She doesn't have a moment to call her own some days.'

Ann was one of those women who had the gift of involving others in whatever she was doing. She would have made a first-rate headmistress, Diana reflected humorously, as she allowed herself to be gently bullied into going with her.

In the event, the meeting proved quite interesting. In addition to Kath Fielding, the Vicar's wife, there were half a dozen other women present including representatives from the Mothers' Union, the Women's Guild, and the Gardening Society; and Diana soon found herself elected to take charge of the overall organisation of the fête with a responsibility to report back to Kath Fielding as and when necessary.

'You've no idea what a burden you've lifted from my shoulders,' Kath confided a little later when only Diana and Ann were left. 'With so many different groups involved, each wanting to outdo the other it can get a little wearing, and as the Vicar's wife, I'm supposed to remain completely impartial—believe me, Solomon had it easy.'

They all laughed, including Diana, who commented, 'I'm not sure I like the sound of that.'

'Don't worry about it, you'll be able to be much firmer with them than I can. Watch out for Marie Philips, she'll try and railroad you into allowing the Women's Guild extra stalls and that always causes problems with the Mothers' Union.'

'And don't worry that you'll be expected to take on any physical work—that side of it will be organised by the men. Diana's expecting,' Ann explained to Kath.

'Are you? How lovely! I miss our two now that

they're grown up and living away from home, although of course it's a terrible shame that your husband won't be here to share the pleasure with you.'

As always, Diana felt extremely uncomfortable at the mention of her imaginary husband. It made her feel guilty to be on the receiving end of so much sympathy and concern when she did not truly merit it, but fortunately Kath put her reticence down to the fact that she found it too upsetting to talk about her husband, and changed the subject.

Was it always going to be like this? Diana wondered later as she prepared for bed. Was she always going to have this guilty feeling that she was deceiving people and cheating her own child? But what alternative did she have? If she told Marcus the truth he might try to take her child away from her, or worse still, he might let her keep it, but try to involve himself in their lives in some way.

She had been forced to revise her opinion of him. She was coming to realise that, far from being the uncaring macho type who jumped into bed with any female who made herself available, he was a deeply caring human being, who would never allow her to keep his child away from him.

At first, she had thought he was pursuing her simply because she was sexually convenient, but now she suspected that she had been wrong; that there was more to it than that and that he actually cared for her as a person; as a woman. But how could that be? He was so unlike the brittle selfish men she was used to that she found it hard to understand him. She was drawn to him both physically and emotionally, but it would be too dangerous to allow those feelings to develop; she had to curb them now. She told herself that she simply wanted someone to love, someone to fill the emptiness of her life, but her child would fill that space. She didn't need anyone else.

She drifted off to sleep, her mind a jumble of unhappy and conflicting thoughts.

In the morning she didn't feel much better. Guilt lingered like a nasty taste in the mouth, clouding her previous happiness.

Today the decorators started work, and she wanted to be there when they arrived. After an early breakfast she made her way on foot down to the house.

The scent of new wood still hung on the air.

She saw the decorators' van draw up outside from an upstairs window, and went down slowly to let them in. A cheery red-headed man in white overalls introduced himself as the 'leader of the gang'.

'I'm Roger, and these other two lackeys are Judy and Phil respectively.'

Judy was a small gamine-faced girl with the shortest haircut Diana had ever seen, while Phil was extremely tall and thin with a worried-looking face.

Diana had already approved the sketches of the mural submitted to her, and she showed the small band into the downstairs shop, pointing out the area where the children's books would be sold.

'Great, I'll leave you to make a start down here while I check out the rest of the house.'

Roger gave Diana a winning smile as she led him upstairs to her own quarters. 'I'm told that you want to keep everything simple up here, in keeping with the age and style of the building. Soft magnolia on the walls and ceilings, that sort of thing.'

'That's right. I felt that wallpaper would be out of place here, and much as I love all the new paint finishes, I don't feel they're right for this particular building.'

'Wise of you,' Roger agreed. 'You must have very strong willpower. Most of our clients do it the other way round; they say, "I know that periodically it isn't quite right, but I love it so much".'

Was she strong-willed? She digested his comment in silence. Perhaps she was, but surely that wasn't a bad thing for a woman living on her own with a child to bring up. She would *need* to be strong-willed.

She went back downstairs with Roger and watched as the other two started outlining the mural. Already the strong smell of paint was beginning to make her feel nauseous, and so she excused herself. She might as well drive into Hereford and check up on the progress the shop was making with her curtains. She still hadn't made up her mind about new bedding and furniture for her bedroom. Ann had mentioned to her a firm that specialised in reproduction furniture of all types. They had a small factory on the outskirts of Hereford that the public were welcome to visit. She would have to ask her exactly where it was. On impulse, instead of driving straight to Hereford, she detoured to the attractive farmhouse where Ann lived with her husband and children. In addition to the house they owned a substantial number of outbuildings and two small paddocks. Theirs was an ideal situation for a busy country vet. Her husband worked from one of the converted barns. Several cars were already drawn up outside in the courtyard. Diana parked alongside them and made her way to the house.

Ann answered the door on her second knock, beaming

from ear to ear when she saw her.

'Come in. You're looking very well. She looks blooming, doesn't she, Marcus?' she called over her shoulder.

It was too late to leave now, she would have to go in. Blessing the darkness of the kitchen, Diana prayed that Ann hadn't noticed the way her colour changed. Of all the bad luck! The last thing she had anticipated was that she might run into Marcus.

'I can't stay,' she told Ann quickly. 'I just called to ask you if you could let me have directions for that furniture place you were telling me about. I'm on my way to Hereford.'

'There you are, Marcus, your prayers have been answered. Marcus called round to ask me if I could go into Hereford to collect Ma's prescription. The local chemist is out of her tablets, and she can't sleep without them. They've got a bit of a crisis on at the farm, and Marcus can't leave. Three of his cows are calving. Michael's over there now. He was hoping that I could go into Hereford for him, but I can't—not right now, I've promised to collect and look after someone else's kids after school, and even if I left now I wouldn't be back in time.'

With a sinking heart, Diana recognised that there was no way she could refuse to help. With the utmost reluctance she took the prescription Ann was handing her, guilt mingling with anger. She had been dreading seeing Marcus again after yesterday. She knew she had behaved unkindly towards him; not only did she feel guilty, she also felt wretchedly mean as well, doubly so when she remembered how brave and cheerful his mother was.

'There's no need to drag Diana into this.'

Diana heard the terseness in his voice as Marcus stepped into the light. The sight of him shocked her. He looked as though he badly needed a shave. His face was drawn with exhaustion, haggard almost, his eyes nearly black in the tired pallor of his face.

Her expression must have betrayed her shock because he rubbed a hand over his jaw and grimaced wryly.

'He's been up all night with his cows,' Ann informed her. 'They're a new breed he's been experimenting with—Charolais—only they're having problems birthing their calves. He's lost three of them already.'

'Thanks, Ann, but I'm sure Diana isn't interested in the fate of my livestock,' Marcus interrupted flatly. 'Which reminds me, I'd better get back. I'll just collect the stuff that Michael wanted from his surgery and then I'll be on my way.'

He paused several feet away from Diana, and she had the feeling that for some reason he didn't want to come any closer to her. It was almost as though he was deliberately keeping a distance between them. But then, why shouldn't he after the way she had behaved yesterday?

She found herself caught in the middle of two conflicting emotions. Part of her was relieved that he was taking her rejection so matter-of-factly, but part of her also felt bereft, betrayed almost, by his patent indifference to her.

He sidestepped past her to reach the door, and within minutes Diana heard the noise of a car engine.

'Poor Marcus, things haven't been going at all well for him recently,' Ann sighed. 'Really he never wanted to take on the farm, you know. He did it for Ma's sake. Our uncle was very old-fashioned in his ways, and Marcus is trying to drag the farm into the twentieth century.

'I'll just give you those directions. Lucky you, starting completely afresh. There are times when I'd love to re-do this place, but then I see a pair of muddy shoes perched on one of the chairs, and I have second thoughts. I keep promising myself I'll have all the pastels and pretties I want when the kids leave home.'

She wrote down the directions and handed the paper to Diana, pausing slightly before asking, 'Would you mind taking Ma's prescription direct to the farm? It isn't much out of your way and ... well, she said the other day how much she had enjoyed meeting you. This will be the first year she hasn't been on the fête committee, and it's making her feel miserable. Seeing you will help to cheer her up.'

How could she refuse without seeming appallingly churlish? As she stepped out into the yard Ann called after her. 'Don't forget dinner on Saturday, will you?'

She found the factory without too much difficulty, and after touring their workshop she was determined to buy something from them. She had fallen in love with a traditional kitchen table, and had also been tempted by a cupboard that they were making to order for another customer. Something like that in her bedroom, it was large enough to take it. But that still didn't solve the problem of somewhere to hang her clothes. There was plenty of room in the dressing-room, which linked her bedroom and bathroom, for wardrobes to be fitted, but she wanted something more in keeping with the house than anything she had seen so far.

When she mentioned this to the man who was showing her round, he beamed with delight.

'No problem at all,' he assured her. 'We could design something specifically to fit your requirements, that will fit in perfectly with the house. I'll show you some photographs of work we've already done on various period bedrooms.'

The photographs he showed her whetted Diana's appetite even further, and before she left she had arranged for him to come out to the house to measure up her dressing-room for a tailor-made period-styled fitted wardrobe.

'Of course, it can't be genuinely authentic, but it will certainly be in keeping with the rest of the building,' she was assured before she left.

In Hereford she was lucky enough to find a parking spot straight away. She visited the chemist first to collect the prescription and then went on to check on the progress of her curtains. They were almost finished, and would be ready to be hung as soon as the decorators had completed their work.

There were men working in the fields as Diana drove homewards. Because of the good weather, farmers were hoping to bring in two crops, and some of the fields were already being cleared for this purpose.

Farming was hard work; how hard she was only just beginning to realise. She thought of Marcus's haggard, exhausted face, and immediately wished she had not, as she felt a renewed upsurge of her earlier guilt. She must stop feeling like this. She had nothing to feel guilty about.

Or had she?

CHAPTER SIX

THE FIELDS around Whitegates Farm were empty of any human occupation. Marcus's Land Rover was parked in the yard, but it was empty of any other vehicles.

Tense with the anticipation of meeting him, Diana climbed out of her own car, clutching the precious prescription. Mrs Jenkins openend the door to her hesitant knock and beamed a welcome at her.

'Well, if that isn't good timing! I was just making Mrs Simons a pot of tea. She'll be delighted that you're here to share it with her. Please, come on through.'

Jane Simons was sitting in her chair on the patio outside her small sitting-room. She smiled welcomingly at Diana.

'It's been such a hot day, I was just trying to catch the early evening breeze. Have you got time to stay and have tea?'

Diana hadn't the heart to refuse. Despite her poised smile, she could see the loneliness in the older woman's eyes.

'Yes, I have. As a matter of fact, I'm glad you asked me. I don't know if Ann's mentioned it, but I've been put in charge of co-ordinating this year's summer fête. I haven't a clue what I should be doing, and Ann just happened to mention to me earlier that you might be able to help me.'

She wasn't strictly telling the truth, but this time her fibs occasioned no guilt at all. It was worth lying just to

see the flush of pleasure and interest colour Jane Simons'
too-thin face.

'You'll need to muster almost all the town before
you've finished,' she warned Diana. 'The marquee will
have been booked already, but it doesn't do any harm
just to check that everything's in order there. Kath will
have a list of telephone numbers for you, and if she
hasn't I should be able to help out. I always keep my old
diaries, and they'll be in there.'

Mrs Jenkins unobtrusively poured the tea, and left
while they were still deep in conversation. Oddly, Diana
felt no sense of unease with Marcus's mother.

'Ann tells me that you're expecting a baby. I did
wonder when you were here before.'

Had she? Diana felt a small frisson of alarm.

'It must be a very poignant time for you: the hope of a
new life combined with the loss of your husband.'

There it was again; that reference to her non-existent
husband, that compassion that she in no way at all
merited.

'This place needs children. I know that Ann's always
nagging Marcus to get married, and I must admit it
would be nice to have another woman around again. My
sister-in-law and I were very good friends, and I still
miss her dreadfully. A son, no matter how loving and
caring, is no substitute for a good woman friend. And
Marcus himself has changed recently; he's become very
preoccupied. I think something's worrying him, but I
don't know what. At first I thought it was the farm, but I
think it's something deeper than that . . . something far
more personal. I'm sorry, my dear.' She gave Diana a
brief smile of apology. 'I must be boring you going on
about my family. Where were we . . .?'

Diana had no alternative but to allow her to change the subject back to the details of the coming fête. It irritated her that she had wanted to hear more about Marcus. She had a mad desire to ask Jane Simons what he had been like as a small child.

What was happening to her? Losing Leslie had made her determined to shun the terrible vulnerability of emotional attachment to another human being.

But it was already too late, she reminded herself; she was already as emotionally committed as it was possible to be, to her unborn child.

Her unborn child. She placed a hand over her stomach.

'My dear, are you all right?'

The concern in Jane Simons' voice brought her out of her deep thoughts.

'I'm fine. I was just . . .'

'Reassuring yourself that you aren't dreaming,' Jane Simons suggested softly. 'I used to do the same, I was so thrilled when I discovered I was expecting Marcus. There is nothing quite like the experience of holding one's first child. Marcus was born here at the farm, because I left it too late to get to the hospital. Poor David was horrified, but he was there with me when Marcus was born. You should have seen his face! You'd think a man who worked as a farmer would be used to the miracle of birth, but when he saw Marcus . . .' She shook her head, smiling gently, and then her expression changed as she looked at Diana's white set face.

'Oh, my dear, forgive me. How tactless . . .'

'No . . . please . . .' Diana stood up clumsily. How could she explain that it wasn't the reference to her husband that had upset her, but the realisation that

Marcus would never look at her child the way his father had looked at him; that her son or daughter would never know the love and tenderness of a father's love. And she was the one who would be depriving him or her of that love . . .

'I must go, it's getting late. They'll be expecting me back at the pub.'

She left the room in a rush, leaving Mrs Jenkins gaping at her as she practically ran to her car.

What on earth *was* the matter with her? She had probably upset Jane Simons with her behaviour, but how could she have told her the truth?

She reached the town in almost record time, berating herself when she realised how fast she had been driving, but instead of going to the pub she stopped her car outside her shop. She had the keys with her, and she wanted to be alone.

The painters had finished for the day and left. The smell of fresh paint hung heavily on the air, but this time it did not make her feel bilious.

She went into the house first, via the rear entrance. True to his promise, Roger had stuck rigidly to the traditional, and now the newly plastered walls had been softened by several applications of thick creamy-white paint that threw into relief the richness of the beams.

Slowly, she made her way downstairs. The smell of paint here was stronger than in the shop, and she held her breath in delight as she saw how well the mural was taking shape. Already she could see the outline of a fairytale castle, a dragon, and a moated drawbridge in the background. In the foreground were the shapes of tiny animals, hidden behind and among toadstools, and an enormous tree. She touched one of the tiny creatures, and found to her shock that she was crying.

These abrupt emotional swings were so alien to her that they continually shocked her. She wiped away the tears with the flat of her hands, tensing as she suddenly heard someone come in through the rear of the building.

She knew before the door opened who it would be. A feeling of inevitability held her in thrall, unable to move. Marcus too stood still, framed in the open doorway, his glance going from her pale wet face, to the newly painted wall.

'My mother was worried about you. She said she had upset you ... something about your husband.'

'No ... no she didn't upset me. I ...' To her horror she felt fresh tears well in her eyes.

Marcus moved, taking her in his arms, and for a moment she allowed herself the luxury of leaning against him. This was wrong; she knew it was wrong, but the temptation was too much for her.

He felt her move.

'Why are you always trying to hold me at a distance?' he demanded fiercely. 'What have I done?'

How could she explain?

She shook her head, 'Nothing ... it's not you ... Marcus ... please go ... I can't explain.'

'You don't have to. It's guilt, isn't it?'

His intuitiveness stunned her, and for one appalled moment she thought he knew everything, but then he went on quietly, 'You feel guilty because we made love so soon after your husband's death.'

He still hadn't let her go. His hands curled round her upper arms, but there was nothing threatening in the way he held her.

'I think I can understand how you feel. You made love

to me out of despair, as a challenge to death. You thought we'd never meet again. But we have met, and there's no reason for you to feel guilty. I still want you, Diana. I think I want you more than any woman I've ever met, but you're deliberately holding me away.'

He was so close to the truth that she panicked.

'Hasn't it occurred to you yet that I simply might not find you attractive enough to repeat what for me was just a one-night stand?' she demanded nastily. 'You seem to have gone very deeply into the supposedly psychological reasons for my behaviour that night, but what makes you think you were the only one, for all you know I . . .'

'Might jump into bed with every man who crosses your path?' he said harshly. 'I don't think so, somehow. That night when I made love to you it was almost like making love to a virgin, or a woman who hadn't had sex in a long, long time.' He said it almost under his breath as though he were talking to himself and not to her. 'And every time I try to talk about it you back off. What are you so afraid of, Diana?'

'Maybe I'm scared of being blackmailed into repeating the experience. Or hasn't that occurred to you yet?'

His face went white, his mouth thinning angrily. 'You honestly think that? No, I don't believe it. You know damn well that . . .'

'That what, Marcus?' she challenged him. 'I don't know you any more than you know me. We're two strangers who went to bed together, that's all; and as far as I'm concerned our night together is something I want to forget.'

'Well, I damn well don't!' He was angry now. She had hurt his pride, and perhaps more. 'And I think you're lying. You might want to forget that night but you can't, can you?' He was almost whispering now, his voice a seductive lure, tormenting her with memories she would rather forget. He had spoken to her in that same soft, sensually aware voice that night. She shivered suddenly, remembering how she had felt.

'Marcus, this is ridiculous.' The words came out on a high, frightened note. 'I don't know why you're doing this.'

'You don't?' He cast her a disbelieving, mocking look. 'Well, then, perhaps I'd better show you.'

She ought to have moved while she had still had the chance, because now it was gone and her body was pressed up against the wall, hemmed in by his. She could feel its heat, and against her will her own flesh responded to the enticement of it. She could feel her muscles compressing as she fought to control her feelings.

'Do you remember how it felt when I touched you like this, Diana? And like this?' His fingertips trailed up her bare arm and her skin quivered. She had an almost unbearable need to reach out and touch him. His short-sleeved shirt bared his arms and revealed his tanned throat. Dark hair curled vibrantly at the parting of the white cloth and she shivered in sexual awareness of his masculinity. What was it about this man that made her so sensually responsive to him?

'You want me.'

He was whispering the words against her lips making panic storm through her.

'No——' Her denial sounded weak and unconvincing even to her own ears.

'Yes.'

She could feel the warmth of his breath. 'Just give me

a chance to prove to you how good it could be between us, Diana.'

Her throat locked, making it impossible for her to speak. His mouth caressed hers, slowly and lingeringly. Her lips parted without any attempt to stop him, and she shuddered beneath the delicate touch of his tongue-tip as it moved tantalisingly against her mouth.

The sensuous torment closed her mind to everything else. Her arms crept up around Marcus's neck, her fingertips stroking the soft hair at his nape. She felt his chest expand as he breathed harshly in response to her touch, and her breasts were flattened against the hard wall of muscle.

'Marcus.' She moaned his name into his open mouth in a plea that needed no interpretation. Her body was saying what her lips could not.

She wanted him, desperately, urgently, she wanted him as she had wanted him that night at the hotel. He moved, supporting her weight against his own, while his fingers deftly unfastened the buttons on her blouse.

The sheer delight of having his hand against her skin was indescribable. Her breast swelled into his palm, the nipple already erect. She heard him stifle a harsh sound of pleasure in his throat as his mouth returned to hers, and that small betraying sound added to her own arousal.

She wanted him; she wanted his hands and mouth on her skin; she wanted his body within her own, she wanted *him*. She clung wildly to him, breathing unsteadily, keeping her eyes tightly closed as her head fell back against his arm, revealing the soft vulnerability of her throat to his eyes and lips.

She shuddered intensely beneath the velvet scorch of

his mouth as it moved over her tender skin. A pulse jumped madly at the base of her throat, and he touched it with his tongue and then his mouth as though he wanted to drink from the life force that pulsed there.

The touch of his hands and mouth was unbearably erotic, but it wasn't enough. She wanted more; she wanted ... A small sob tore at her clenched throat muscles, and as though he understood her need, his body moved even closer to her own, his muscled thigh moving between her own trembling legs.

The weight and heat of him offered a brief panacea to her need, but it didn't last long. She arched pleadingly against him, and cried out in savage, fierce pleasure as his mouth found the peak of her breast, and drew fiercely on it.

Her head buzzed, her heart was thudding, her body was on fire with arousal and desire.

'Marcus ...'

'Yes ... Yes ...'

His voice reached her, thick and unfamiliar. His hands trembled where they touched her skin.

Outside in the street a car backfired, and abruptly Diana came to her senses. With a soft cry of pain she pushed Marcus away from her, quickly covering up her half-naked body.

'Diana ...'

She felt sick with self-disgust and embarrassment. 'Please go, Marcus ...'

Even her voice was trembling.

'No, damn it, I won't. I want to know what it is that makes you keep on rejecting me, when we both know that you want me as much ...'

'No!' The tortured denial was ripped from her throat,

leaving it raw with pain. 'No . . . You *made* me want you, Marcus. I . . .'

He ignored the trembled words, swearing savagely. 'Like hell! You wanted me . . . just like you wanted me that first night.'

'No . . . No . . . I *hate* you, Marcus.'

It was the cry of a lost child, and she saw his mouth twist with the comprehension of that fact.

'Why?' he taunted. 'Because I can make you forget your husband? Do you know what I'd like to do, Diana? I'd like to make you forget that any other man existed.'

The vehemence in his voice stunned her.

'I'd like to make you forget everything but how you feel when I touch you. I'd like to make you forget . . .'

'That I'm carrying another man's child.' She had to stop him, she couldn't endure much more.

She saw his face go white, and watched the bleakness sear his eyes. 'I have a commitment to my child, Marcus. I can't enter into an affair with you—I don't even want to. I've already told you that. In future, please, leave me alone.'

She turned her back on him, and bit deeply into her bottom lip to stop herself from calling back the words.

'I came here tonight intending to apologise for what I said to you the last time we met here,' Marcus said slowly. 'But it doesn't matter *what* I do or say, does it, Diana? You're determined to keep me out of your life. Is that really what you think your husband would have wanted? Was he really the kind of man who would want you to live like a nun for the rest of your life?'

'What makes you think I intend to?' Diana lashed back bitterly. 'You're so arrogant, Marcus. You seem to

think that just because you want me, I should want you
in return.'

'You *do* want me.'

'No,' she lied brutally. 'I just want a man—any man.
It's something to do with the baby. It affects me that
way.'

'You're lying.'

She had the feeling that if she moved he would spring
at her like a wild animal. For the first time since she had
known him she felt frightened of him. She had pushed
him too far. In her fear of betraying herself she had said
too much. She turned her head away from him, unable
to speak, trembling with fear and anguish. A single tear
formed and ran down her cheek.

'My God, what are we doing to each other?'

She heard the anguish in Marcus's voice and felt
shamed by it. She was the one who was to blame for this.
She was the one responsible.

'I'm going now, but I'm not going to give up,' he
warned her. 'Somehow there must be a way of getting
through to you; of proving to you that life goes on. I
know you want me, Diana, and whatever you say, I know
you're no wanton.'

'Why . . .?' she cried out in anguish. 'Why me? Why
not one of the girls that Ann keeps throwing at you?'

'I wish I knew,' he told her sombrely. 'All I do know is
that there hasn't been a single night since we met when I
haven't woken up and longed to have you in my arms.'

She realised as she heard him leave that what he had
just said was true for her as well. She had fought against
knowing it, against admitting it even to herself, but it
was true. She wasn't sure yet what she felt for him, but

what she did know was that it must be ruthlessly and instantly crushed.

Only it wasn't as easy as that, as she soon discovered. It was Kath who told her that Marcus would be in charge of the men responsible for setting up and providing the equipment for the fête.

'It makes sense, of course, since we're using his land. You'll find him a terrific help.'

She didn't *want* his help, she told herself rebelliously as she walked back from the Vicarage. It was Friday afternoon, and by evening the decorators should be finished.

Tomorrow she was having dinner with Ann and her husband, and it suddenly struck her that she had nothing fit to wear. Her pregnancy was really beginning to show now, and it was time she bought some proper maternity clothes. If only she could have got out of this dinner, but it was impossible to back down now.

It was six o'clock before the decorators finished. Roger came up to the pub to take Diana down for a final inspection of their work.

The mural was an undeniable work of art. Cheeky-faced rabbits and other woodland creatures peeped from behind toadstools; a fiercely frowning dragon fought valiantly against a knight in armour; a flight of crazy stairs led over the drawbridge and into the castle. A wicked-looking witch peeped from one corner, where she tended her bubbling cauldron.

On the opposite wall, another mural depicted scenes from outer space for the more sophisticated tastes; laser beams and space craft of all types filled the darkness of deep space. Diana gazed at the walls in silence.

'Well?' Roger asked her.

'It's fabulous—just what I wanted. The only problem is, the kids are going to be too busy looking at the murals to pay attention to the books.'

The idea of having the murals had originally been that they would capture the children's attention, and allow their parents to browse, but now Diana hoped that what they saw on the walls would spark off a desire to read about what they were looking at.

'It really is fabulous,' she praised the waiting trio. 'I can't tell you how pleased I am.'

After they had gone she went over the house from top to bottom. Only one room had wallpaper—the nursery—and she had chosen a soft pastel-coloured paper with a nursery frieze. Roger had painted a deep blue sky ceiling with clouds floating on it to match up with the wallpaper. It was too soon yet to buy any nursery furniture, but she already knew what she wanted.

On Monday her carpets were being laid, and later in the week the curtains and furniture would arrive. By next weekend she should be in, and then she could concentrate on sorting out the shop. Already the store room at the back was getting filled with boxes of books. She would have to put an ad. in the local paper for an assistant; perhaps a girl not long out of school.

She walked back to the pub, and was just on the point of entering her room when the landlady caught up with her.

'There's a message from Ann for you. She said to tell you that Mr Simons would pick you up tomorrow evening, to save you driving.'

Diana went cold all over. What on earth was Ann trying to do? She longed to pick up the phone and cancel the whole thing, but how could she? Was Ann attempting another matchmaking exercise? She almost ground her teeth with impatience. Every time she saw Marcus it seemed to weaken her willpower. Every time she saw him she ached to tell him the truth. Sometimes she even found herself fantasising about what his reaction would be if she did. Part of her wanted to lean on him, she realised; part of her yearned for that close communication they had shared; part of her wanted him to share her joy in their coming child, but it was only a very, very tiny part. She didn't really want any sort of commitment with anyone else. Losing Leslie had hurt too much for her to risk losing anyone again. Perhaps she was being illogical, but that was the way she felt, and nothing could change it.

She had made love with Marcus on a wave of intense emotion that had blotted out everything else, and deep within her lingered the fear that somehow Marcus himself could still conjure that emotion.

She didn't want that. She wanted to live her life free of the pain that came with loving.

But she was carrying his child. A child she already loved. That was different, she told herself stubbornly; loving her child was safe in a way that loving Marcus would not be.

Loving him. She shivered and pushed the thought away.

CHAPTER SEVEN

MARCUS arrived right on the stroke of eight. From her bedroom window, Diana saw the Daimler drive into the car park and stop.

When Marcus got out her heart all but turned over. He was dressed formally in a dinner suit, its darkness reminding her almost unbearably of the first time they had met. He had been dressed formally then, too.

Almost as though he could sense her watching him he looked upwards. She stepped back from the window immediately.

She was wearing a new dress. A floaty creation in soft pastel-hued silks that she had bought that afternoon from a rather up-market maternity boutique she had discovered tucked down a side-street in Hereford.

In addition to the dress, she had bought herself two pairs of serviceable dungarees from Mothercare, and some comfortable flat shoes.

Her pregnancy was only just beginning to show noticeably, and the cleverly cut panels of the dress were flattering. Its short sleeves revealed her tanned arms, her hair seemed to shine with a new lustre, and her face glowed. She looked the epitome of a healthily and happily pregnant woman, Diana knew, and if it wasn't for Marcus she knew that she would be.

She went downstairs to meet him with great reluctance. He was waiting for her at the bottom of the stairs. His smile was friendly, but nothing more.

117

What had she expected? she asked herself as he escorted her out to his car. That he would take her into his arms and start to kiss her passionately in front of everyone?

She went automatically to the front passenger door of the car only to realise that it was the rear door that Marcus was holding open for her.

Puzzled, she got inside, and then realised that she and Marcus weren't travelling alone.

A pretty blonde-haired girl sat in the front passenger seat. She turned round to smile at Diana and introduce herself.

'Hi! I'm Patty Dewar. I've heard all about you from Ann and my folks.'

'Patty's parents are old friends of Ann's. You'll meet them tonight. Patty's father is our local solicitor.'

Patty wrinkled her delightfully *retroussé* nose and flashed Marcus a sweetly ingenuous smile. She couldn't be a day over twenty-one, Diana thought acidly, but even so, surely the wide-eyed *ingenue* act was overdone. She looked at the slim, pretty hand clinging to Marcus's arm, and was shocked at the wave of dislike that ran through her.

'I'm just home on a flying visit. I'm at drama school— RADA. Daddy nearly blew a fuse when I told him I wanted to act, but luckily Mummy was all for it. If darling Marcus hadn't come to my rescue tonight I'd have had to stay in moping. He's such a sweetie-pie.' She blew a kiss in Marcus's direction, while Diana looked on, totally bemused by her own feelings of irrational jealousy. Marcus had a perfect right to date whoever he wished. Only yesterday she had been privately bemoaning the fact that his attention seemed to be focused on her, but now that he had so obviously found consolation elsewhere, she found herself bitterly resenting the presence of the other girl.

'I was supposed to be flying to the South of France this weekend with some friends, but it was cancelled at the last moment, so I came home instead. When Marcus heard that I was all alone there, he insisted on bringing me with him.'

She batted eyelashes which could never in a million years have been natural, in Marcus's direction.

It was true that he seemed totally unmoved by her kittenish behaviour; phlegmatic would have been the closest description to his unreadable expression, but he had quite obviously invited the girl to partner him tonight.

She ought to be pleased that he had finally decided to give up pursuing her, Diana told herself. Only she wasn't; she felt both jealous and resentful of the other girl's presence, and for the first time she was conscious of the clumsiness of her pregnant body, when compared to the lithe slenderness of the girl in the front seat. Only five years or so separated them, but she made Diana feel like Methuselah.

Her artless chit-chat was full of references to people that Diana didn't know, and peppered with 'do you remembers', including the cleverly revealed fact that there had been occasions when Marcus had dated her when he was in London.

'I was so sorry to miss you the last time you were up, darling, but it was unavoidable.'

Swivelling round in her seat, she said to Diana, 'Marcus sometimes goes to London in his role as local representative for the farmers round here. We normally manage to get together, but the last time he was up I was away with friends. Did you miss me?'

Her fingers stroked down his black sleeve, and Diana found herself gritting her teeth. If nothing else surely it was dangerous to distract Marcus from his driving like that.

Not that he showed any sign of being distracted, she noticed, other than a small smile.

When he made no reply, Patty pouted and said sulkily, 'I suppose that means you didn't. Honestly, Marcus, you're incorrigible. I suppose you picked up some horsy type and spent the whole evening flirting outrageously with her,' she accused nastily. 'Marcus is the most appalling flirt, you know,' she threw over her shoulder to Diana. 'But I suppose you've already learned that.'

Was that a warning?

'Not really,' Diana responded coolly, permitting a rather tight smile to curl her mouth as she added, 'We hardly know one another well enough for me to make such judgments.'

In the driving-mirror she saw Marcus looking sardonically at her, and she could feel herself starting to flush. Damn him, why did he have to make her so painfully aware of him, and what they had shared?

As though one unpleasant shock wasn't enough, Diana discovered when they arrived at Ann's that contrary to her expectation she had been paired off with a widower friend of her hosts.

Ian Michaels was a pleasant enough man, but he was well into his fifties, and his conversation was limited to his business dealings. Diana found her glance straying almost continuously to the group which included Patty and Marcus.

Ann came up to her at one point and smiled when she saw where she was looking.

'Patty used to have the most dreadful crush on Marcus. He was so patient with her. She's outgrown it now, of course, but I think it's rather floored Marcus to discover what a very pretty girl she's grown into. He's just at that age as well when he could easily fall for someone pretty and giddy.'

Diana didn't know what to say. Her throat had gone dry and seemed to be blocked by a hugely painful lump. She wanted nothing more than to run out of Ann's drawing-room and not come back.

She felt as bereft and miserable as a child suddenly deserted by its parents. Where only yesterday she had demanded that Marcus leave her alone, now she longed for his presence at her side. She was behaving like a dog in a manger, she derided herself, but knowing it didn't help. She was still perversely jealous and resentful of Patty's presence at his side.

Ian Michaels kept up his monologue throughout the meal, with Diana interposing the odd word here and there. What made her feel worse was that everyone else seemed to be enjoying themselves.

The dining-room was large enough to seat a dozen people, and Ann was obviously an experienced hostess. The conversation flowed around her, leaving her feeling excluded and alone. She told herself that it was her own fault for not joining in, but every time she took her attention off Ian, all she could hear was Patty's light chatter, and Marcus's deeper response. Because she wasn't using her own car, she was even denied the time-honoured excuse of leaving early because she wasn't feeling well.

After dinner everyone congregated in the drawing-room, where Ann served coffee, assisted by her eldest daughter. Patty perched provocatively on the arm of Marcus's chair, and since they were sitting right opposite her, she could not even avoid looking at them.

'You look dreadfully tired,' Patty called out to her as Ann served their coffee. 'Poor you, pregnancy is such a dreadful strain on a woman, isn't it? I should hate to be on my own with the sole responsibility for my child. And, of course, it isn't every man who will take on another man's child, is it?'

There was a small, rather charged silence, broken only when Mrs Dewar said in a flustered voice, 'Patty, really ...' She cast an apologetic and embarrassed glance at Diana and said, 'I'm awfully sorry about that. Patty never stops to think before she speaks.'

Diana longed to be able to reply truthfully, and tell Sally Dewar that, contrary to her words, it was her own private belief that Patty had known exactly what she was saying.

Were there other people who thought she was looking for a husband—any husband? Her mouth tightened slightly, and she got up. Ann had gone back to the kitchen to refill the coffee-pot and Diana followed her there.

Fortunately, Ann was alone.

'I'm awfully sorry, but I'm afraid I'll have to leave. Patty is quite right, being pregnant is draining. I don't want to disturb anyone else, so could I ring for a taxi?'

'Oh, there's no need for that, Marcus will take you home.'

Diana shook her head firmly. 'No . . . I don't want to disturb him.'

She felt the door open behind her, and swung round half expecting to see Marcus, but instead she saw the plump shape of Ian Michaels standing in the doorway.

'I'm afraid I'm going to have to leave, Ann, my dear,' he apologised. 'I've got an early flight to Paris in the morning.'

'Oh, Ian, you're just in the nick of time. Diana wants to leave, too. She's feeling rather tired, and she's on your way . . .'

Diana wanted to protest, but she sensed that if she did Ann would insist on Marcus taking her home, and that was the last thing she wanted. She could just imagine Patty Dewar's reaction if Marcus was dragged away from *her* to escort her home, and so she had no alternative but to reluctantly follow Ian Michaels out to his car.

The return journey was a silent one. Ian Michaels was obviously preoccupied with his coming business trip. He dropped her off outside the pub, and opened the car door for her. It was obvious that he had relished being paired off with her as little as she had with him.

'Don't worry about it,' he told her kindly. 'Ann means well. She's so happily married herself she can't understand why everyone else shouldn't be paired up as well. I loved my wife very much—so much that I don't have any desire to replace her.'

He immediately went up in Diana's estimation. She had thought previously that he hadn't been aware of Ann's good-natured machinations, but obviously he had, and by talking about them, he had lessened her own sense of angry embarrassment.

As she lay in bed waiting for sleep, she found herself doubting that Marcus would simply drop Patty off outside her front door when he eventually took her home.

The intensity of her sense of jealousy and loss frightened her. She had no right to feel jealous. No right at all . . . and no reason. She felt nothing for Marcus. Nothing? For the father of her child? Was that what she was going to tell her child when it was old enough to start asking questions? That she had felt nothing for its father?

Too confused to pursue the thought any further, she buried her head in her pillow and willed herself to fall asleep.

By Tuesday, when she had still not seen Marcus, she told herself that she was glad that Patty was obviously keeping him otherwise engaged.

The carpets had arrived and been laid, and very attractive they looked too, but she was discovering that the pleasure wasn't as great when there was no one to share it with. Before, there had always been Leslie, or before that, her family.

She sighed faintly to herself as she went from room to room admiring the pale grey floor covering.

Only that morning she had received a letter from her mother; telling her that her sister-in-law was expecting her third child.

Of course, her parents were overjoyed, and her mother had written that Sandra was desperately hoping that this baby would be a boy, since they already had two girls. The letter contained a vague suggestion that she should go out for a holiday, but her brother had always been closer to their parents than she was herself.

Some time they would have to know about her baby; but not just yet. She sat down to write back and was amazed to discover how quickly she covered several sheets. Normally she had very little to write to them about, and she wondered how it was that while living such a quiet life in the country, as opposed to her busy life in London, she should have so much more to write about.

Perhaps it was because here she knew people on a different level. Here for instance, she knew all about Mrs Gibbs in the Post Office's family, and about her rheumatism; she knew how much Madge Davies, the landlady of the pub, missed her daughter who was away at university. She knew the intimacies of people's lives in a way that had been impossible when she lived in London.

The letter written and posted, she decided she might as well do some work on the preparations for the fête. It would keep her mind busy ... stop her from thinking about Marcus.

There was nothing further she could do on the shop until the rest of her stock arrived. Her ad. was due to go into the following week's paper.

The marquee hire firm confirmed that everything was in order from their end, when Diana telephoned them.

'I suppose that as in previous years you'll provide your own generators?' the Manager asked her.

Diana was flummoxed. She knew nothing at all about the generators. Telling him that she would look into it, she went through Jane Simons' extremely comprehensive lists once again.

She found the word 'generators' written at the bottom

on a long list of things, with an asterisk marking it. What did the asterisk mean?

Biting her lip Diana studied the list again and could come up with no explanation. She would have to telephone the farm.

She looked up through the window and saw that the sun was shining. Suddenly, she was tired of being cooped up indoors. Instead of telephoning she would drive out there.

So that you can see Marcus, an inner voice taunted, but she silenced it. Of course she wouldn't see Marcus, he would be out working on the farm, and besides, she didn't want to see him. Patty Dewar was welcome to him.

That didn't stop her heart from lurching betrayingly half an hour later when she drove into the farm yard, and saw the Land Rover parked there.

She was being stupid, she told herself. Other men besides Marcus were bound to drive the farm vehicle, and besides, why should she feel this absurd flutter of panicky excitement? She didn't want to see him . . . did she?

Mrs Jenkins, normally so efficient, seemed to take a long time to answer the door. When she did arrive she looked flushed and worried, although her face cleared a little when she saw Diana.

'Oh, thank goodness someone's here,' she cried worriedly. 'Its Mrs Simons, she's fallen out of her chair. I only found her when I went to take her morning cup of coffee to her. I didn't dare touch her. I've rung the doctor, but he's out on a call . . . and Ann has gone to Hereford. I've sent one of the men looking for Marcus. He's out supervising some work right on the other side of the farm. Perhaps with the two of us we could get Mrs Simons back in her chair.'

Diana frowned worriedly as she followed the housekeeper inside. 'Would that be wise? Ought we to touch her, I mean? Couldn't we just make her more comfortable? Where is she?'

'In her sitting-room.'

Jane Simons had obviously fallen as she reached out to open her patio door. She lay in a crumpled heap on the floor beside her chair. There was a nasty bruise forming on her temple, and although she was unconscious, there were no signs of any other damage.

'I think we should just ease a cushion under her head, and put a blanket over her, in case she's in shock,' Diana suggested. 'She seems to be breathing normally.'

She squatted on the floor trying to remember her own smattering of first aid training. Wasn't it important to keep the victim's air passage clear? That didn't seem to be a problem in Mrs Simons' case; she seemed to be breathing quite well.

'What did you say to the doctor's receptionist?'

'I told her what had happened and asked her to get in touch with Dr Thomas as soon as possible.'

'If he's out on a call, perhaps we ought to ring for an ambulance ...'

Mrs Jenkins seemed to have gone completely to pieces, but now, obviously reassured by Diana's calm presence, she was starting to recover. While Diana sat with Mrs Simons, Mrs Jenkins went to ring for an ambulance. When she came back, she brought Diana a cup of tea.

'Is there any change?'

Diana shook her head. Once or twice Jane Simons had

moaned and moved her head, but apart from that here had been no sign of returning consciousness.

The farm seemed broodingly silent and for the first time it struck Diana that it was quite remote. She shivered in the cool breeze from the open window, and tucked the blanket more firmly round Marcus's mother.

Her ears had been straining for so long to catch the sound of a vehicle, that when she did hear it, she thought she was imagining things; but the noise grew stronger, and relief flooded through her as she heard the engine stop and a door open.

Marcus was wearing jeans and a checked shirt. There were smears of dirt across his face and arms, and he hadn't stopped to remove his outdoor boots.

Ignoring everyone but his mother, he dropped down on his haunches beside her, quickly checking her pulse, and flicking back her eyelids.

'It's just concussion, I think—thank God! When I got Rab's message, I thought for a moment she might have had a stroke.'

He had barely finished speaking when simultaneously an ambulance siren and the doctor's car arrived.

Dr Thomas wasted no time in pleasantries, but Diana noticed that despite his brusque manner he was extraordinarily gentle with his patient, pronouncing much the same verdict as Marcus.

'I want her in hospital of course, just to make sure. Marcus?'

'I'm coming with you.'

He got up and frowned, suddenly seeming to realise that Diana was there. He looked at her as though unable to comprehend why, and she explained quickly the business that had brought her to the farm.

'It was a mercy she arrived when she did,' Mrs Jenkins put in. 'I was in a regular panic, I can tell you. I hadn't even thought to ring for an ambulance.'

'I've been afraid of something like this happening,' Marcus said in a low tormented voice. 'I've pleaded with Ma to have a nurse, but she won't. She says that would take away her last little bit of independence.'

'Don't even think about blaming yourself, Marcus.' Dr Thomas interrupted curtly. 'Your mother is a very brave woman, but a stubborn one.'

'I want to be with her when she comes round. You know how she feels about hospitals.'

He was talking to the doctor, but Diana knew that he was referring to the loathing of the institution where she had first learned that she had lost the ability to walk.

'Someone will have to tell Ann. She'll need her things, when she comes round.'

The ambulancemen were already discreetly but carefully putting Mrs Simons on to the stretcher. On impulse Diana said quickly, 'I could stay and do that, Marcus, and I'll ring Ann and explain to her.'

For a moment she thought he was going to reject her offer, and she could feel the hot tide of colour sweep her skin, but after the minutest pause, he said rawly, 'I'll have to accept. I can't leave Mrs Jenkins here on her own. Tell Ann that I'll stay with Ma until she comes round. When the men come back tonight, could you ask Rab—he's the foreman—to keep things ticking over here until I get back? If there's anything urgent he can ring me at the hospital.'

If he was going to stay with his mother until she came round he would need a change of clothes, and his razor; and while Marcus followed the stretcher out to the

ambulance, Diana quickly asked Mrs Jenkins to pack an
overnight bag of necessities for him.

'Oh, and some sandwiches, and a flask of coffee if
we've got time. I'll do that. He won't want anything
right now, but later ...'

It was all done within five minutes, and Diana thrust
the bag and its contents into Marcus's arms just as he
was about to get into the ambulance.

'I'll need someone to come and pick me up eventually,
but I can sort that out later. Diana ...' He looked at her
as though he wanted to say something, but the men were
already closing the ambulance doors.

The shock of his mother's accident and its effect on
him had shown Diana what a genuinely caring man he
was. She wanted some of that caring for herself ... she
needed ...

She needed nothing, she told herself firmly. Nothing
at all.

She could quite easily have gone back to town. She
was planning to move into her new home at the
weekend, and there were any number of things she had
to do, but somehow she found herself reluctant to leave.

She excused her weakness on the grounds that Mrs
Jenkins seemed to want her to stay. The housekeeper
was not a young woman, and the accident had obviously
shocked her.

It was Diana who telephoned Ann and gave her the
news. After her initial concern, Ann was all calm
practicality.

'Marcus will stay with Ma until she's safely out of any
danger. I'll ring the hospital and report back to you if
there's any news. Thank goodness you arrived when you
did, Diana. Mrs Jenkins is a darling, but she isn't getting

any younger herself, and she does tend to panic when things go wrong. Marcus will be giving himself a hard time over this. He's been trying to persuade Ma to have a live-in companion, or better still, a nurse, for ages, but she simply won't have it. I'll report back to you just as soon as I've heard anything,' she promised again before she rang off.

When they had heard nothing by evening, apart from a phone call from Ann to say that her mother was still unconscious and undergoing tests, Diana decided that it was time that she left, but the moment she broached the subject Mrs Jenkins begged her to stay.

She had already passed on Marcus's message to his men, and there was nothing for her to linger for. The phone rang just as she was debating the issue. She let Mrs Jenkins answer it, and could tell almost immediately from the housekeeper's reaction that Marcus was on the other end of the line.

'He wants to speak to you,' Mrs Jenkins told her after a few moments' conversation.

'Marcus, your mother ...? was her first anxious enquiry.

'She's recovered consciousness, thank God, and the hospital doesn't think there's been any damage. They want to keep her in overnight though, and I'm going to stay here with her. I just wanted to thank you for everything you've done. Will you tell Mrs J that I'll be back in the morning for milking?'

He was gone before Diana could ask any further questions. She relayed his message to the housekeeper, who looked weepy with relief.

'I really must go now, Mrs Jenkins,' Diana told her

gently, and this time the other woman did not try to stop her.

It was growing dark as she drove along the country lanes, the sky flushed still with the radiance of the dying sunset. With the car window down Diana could breathe in the soft clear air. Now that the initial anxiety was over she could feel herself relaxing.

What amazed her most was how involved she had become with the local community in such a short space of time. Even if Jane Simons had not been Marcus's mother she would still have been worried for her. She admired the older woman tremendously. Hers was not the sort of courage that made headlines in newspapers; it was a more enduring, more heartbreaking courage, a courage that was far harder to maintain.

When she got back to the pub it transpired that they had already heard the news of Jane Simons' accident. She answered Madge Davies' concerned questions as best she could, knowing they sprang from genuine concern and not avid curiosity.

She felt too restless to settle down to anything, and so she walked down to the shop and let herself in. The few possessions she had brought from London were still packed away in a corner of the store-room. Thinking of human endurance and courage had brought Leslie vividly to life in her thoughts.

The house was really ready for occupation now; all the services were laid on, the new bedding she had ordered had been washed and put away. She picked up one of the light boxes and carried it upstairs to her room.

Kneeling down on the floor, she started to unpack it. The very first thing she found was a photograph of Leslie taken the year she graduated. It showed a happy,

smiling girl, with an open, friendly expression and a
mass of dark curly hair.

Diana studied the photograph forlornly for several
minutes. The plastic frame was slightly chipped. She
hadn't noticed that before. Leslie had kept the photograph on her bedside table—to remind her of what she
really was, she had once told Diana on one of her bad
days.

'This sick person lying here isn't really me, you
know,' she had said quietly. 'That's what I tell myself.
That's me ... that girl in the photograph with
everything to look forward to in life.'

After Leslie's death she hadn't been able to bear to
look at the photograph, but now seeing it brought back
the reality of her friend in sharp focus. She found herself
remembering their days at university; the fun they had
had ...

She wiped the glass carefully and stood the photograph up on the deep windowsill.

First thing tomorrow she would go out and buy a
proper silver frame for it.

There were other things in the box. Leslie's GCE
certificates, her degree and the gown she had worn, a
collection of small glass animals she had loved, Diana
found herself weeping softly over them.

The glass animals had been some of Leslie's most
treasured personal possessions. She had collected them
while she was living with her aunt and uncle, and
although they had little monetary value, to Leslie they
had represented the only real warmth and security she
had known as a child.

She would keep them for her own daughter—if she

had one, Diana decided, carefully refolding them in cotton wool.

There were other things; letters from Leslie's solicitor, which she had simply stuffed in the box in her first shock of Leslie's death, and more photographs, casual ones this time, showing the two of them standing with a couple of boyfriends—two boys they had met on holiday one year.

It was the sudden realisation that all the lights had gone out in the street that made Diana realise how late it was. She glanced at her watch shocked to discover that it was after eleven.

Suddenly she felt intensely tired, and she looked longingly at her bed. The new duvet cover was still in its box; it wouldn't take long to unpack it and make up the bed.

On impulse she picked up the phone and dialled the number of the pub. Madge Davies answered it on the first ring, and Diana told her that she had decided to spend the night in her new home.

'I'll be back for breakfast in the morning though, I'm afraid. I don't have any food here yet.'

She had put the water on earlier in the day and it was still hot enough for a quick shower. She had no night clothes with her, but it was a warm night, and both the bed and the duvet were blissfully comfortable. She was asleep within seconds.

It was the sound of someone knocking loudly on the back door that woke her up.

She opened her eyes, thoroughly disorientated, wondering why she wasn't in her room at the pub. It was not even dawn; a thin grey light filtered through the closed curtains.

The knocking from downstairs continued, imperative and urgent. Pulling on her top and skirt, she ran barefoot downstairs and opened the door.

'Marcus!'

Until that moment she hadn't stopped to think who her early morning visitor might be.

'I saw a light on downstairs and the closed curtains. I was just on my way back from the hospital.'

His skin looked grey in the harsh electric light, tired lines raying out from his eyes.

'Your mother?' Diana asked anxiously.

'Improving, thank God, although they're going to keep her in for a couple more days.' He pushed his fingers through his already disturbed hair, looking drained and vulnerable.

'I don't suppose there's any chance of a cup of coffee, is there? Mrs J won't be up yet, and that stuff at the hospital was vile.'

'Come on up. I've got a filter machine in the kitchen—but that's about all at the moment. I'm afraid I can't offer you anything to eat.'

'I'm not hungry.'

As he followed her up the narrow stairs she was intensely conscious of him physically. Half-way up, the baby suddenly kicked—hard—and she stopped abruptly, clutching her stomach with her hands.

From behind her, she heard Marcus call out harshly, 'Diana, for God's sake ... what is it?'

He grabbed hold of her as though he was afraid she was going to pass out, swinging her round to face him.

'It's nothing ... just the baby kicking.'

His eyes followed the line of her body to where her palm rested. Through the thin cotton of her skirt the

impatient movement of the small limb was clearly
discernible, and Diana heard him catch his breath, and
then go so white that she thought he might faint.

'Can I . . .?' He swallowed. 'Can I feel?'

Such an intimate request momentarily threw her. She
would have thought that as a farmer Marcus would be
immune to the wonder of pregnancy and birth, but there
was no mistaking the look of awed fascination in his eyes.

A tiny thrill of pleasure shot through her that he
should want to reach out and touch his child, and, with
an unconsciously Madonna-like smile, she took hold of
his calloused hand and placed it flat against her stomach.

As though he or she knew what was required, the baby
kicked vigorously again.

'The miracle of new life,' Marcus said hoarsely. His
hand dropped away from her and he said abruptly. 'I
thought my mother was going to die. I went through a
hell of guilt while I waited for her to come round, and
the worse thing of all was my fear that somehow she
might will herself not to . . . that she might *want* to die.'

He looked up at her, and Diana saw the unashamed
shimmer of tears in his eyes.

Without conscious thought she leaned forwards and
took him in her arms, his head resting on her breast.

The fact that they were still standing awkwardly on
the stairs was forgotten as their traditional roles were
reversed, and she was the one who gave comfort and he
the one who took it.

As she looked down at his bowed dark head she felt a
surge of emotion so deep, so strong and sure, that it was
almost as though new power and life was flowing into
her body; and then Marcus moved, breaking their
physical contact, and the moment was over.

They went up to her kitchen in silence. Marcus helped her to prepare the coffee, and as it started to drip through the filter she offered awkwardly, 'I think there's some hot water if you want a shower . . .'

It had occurred to her that when he got back to the farm he would have to go straight out to work, and that a shower might help to refresh him a little.

'I'd love one. If you're sure you don't mind?'

'Not at all . . . It's through my bedroom, the door's open, and there are clean dry towels in the cupboard. If you're quick the coffee should just about be ready when you are.'

He hadn't returned when the coffee was ready, so she poured it and waited . . . and waited . . . until, feeling thoroughly alarmed, she hurried up the second flight of stairs to her bedroom.

Marcus was lying sprawled full-length on her bed. He looked as though he had just sat down, and then been completely overcome by exhaustion.

Beads of moisture still clung to his skin, as though he had been in the act of drying himself, and as she looked closer Diana could see that in addition to the towel wrapped round his hips, another damp one lay beneath him.

He would be back for milking, he had told Mrs Jenkins, and it was almost four o'clock now. Indecisively, she stood there. It was clear that he needed his sleep and it was equally clear that he would be annoyed if she didn't wake him.

As she bent uncertainly towards him the decision was taken out of her hands. He opened his eyes and looked up into her face, bemusement turning to such blazing delight as his eyes met hers and registered the reality of her that it made her throat ache.

He reached out and touched her wrist tentatively, and then he smiled at her.

'So you *are* real; this time ...'

'Marcus—the milking—you'll need ...'

'There's only one thing I need right now, and that's you.' His voice was rough and low, and his fingers tightened round her wrist like a vice, to prevent her automatic backward step.

'I want you, Diana. I've dreamed about being with you like this so often. Please don't send me away.'

'Marcus ...'

'No ... No, don't say anything.'

He sat up and took her in his arms before she could stop him. The sheer physical pleasure of being so close to his warm male body silenced all her protests and weakly she found herself responding to the slow, erotic movement of his mouth on her own.

When she did finally manage to pull away her heart was thudding as heavily as his own.

'Marcus, the farm ...'

'What farm?' he demanded huskily, his hold on her tightening, and she knew that she was lost.

Sexually, as well as emotionally, he seemed to spark off a need in her that refused to be denied. She knew that what she was doing was folly, but no matter how logical the arguments against making love with Marcus might be, she knew they were not strong enough to make her send him away.

He lifted her on to the bed beside him and looked into her eyes. His hand touched her stomach gently, caressing the swell of their growing child.

'Will he or she mind?'

The simplicity of the question, the fact that he cared enough about her to ask, filled her with an almost melancholic emotion. What a marvellous father he would have been; still would be to someone else's child ... She reached up and touched his face, gasping as he buried his lips against her open palm, and pleasure stabbed wildly through her.

She ought to send him away. She ought ... but he was lowering her towards the bed, and the sight and scent of him, the feel of his naked weight bearing her back against the mattress awakened such atavistic and pleasurable memories that she simply closed her mind to what she ought to be doing.

It didn't take him long to remove her clothes, but even so both of them were trembling when he eventually touched her skin.

She hadn't realised how deep an imprint he had made upon her senses until now. Her very flesh seemed to welcome him as though it had yearned for his touch.

He caressed every inch of her, exploring her changed shape, pressing tender kisses against the swollen curves of her breasts, until the tiny sound she half suppressed deep in her throat told him that she wanted more than tenderness from him.

Beneath her fingertips Diana felt the smooth mesh of his muscles and then their tension beneath her touch, and she was filled with a deep, feminine sense of power.

In her arms this man became as vulnerable as a child, just as she was vulnerable to him. She shivered, closing her mind to the thought, and shaking her head, when Marcus lifted his to murmur softly, 'Cold?'

'Hold me, Marcus. Just hold me,' she pleaded with him, wrapping her arms tightly around him.

She felt his response to her in the sudden hardening of his body. His mouth burned on hers, his tongue invading her moist sweetness with a thrusting rhythmic movement that echoed the pulsing hunger of his body.

He had wanted her for so long; had dreamed of holding her like this ... when they were together this way it was almost possible to forget that she loved another man and that she carried his child.

The feelings Marcus aroused inside her were impossible to resist. His mouth moved to her throat and she shivered in convulsive pleasure. He kissed her breasts, taking her tender nipples deep into the fierce heat of his mouth, making her cry out as spasms of delight racked her, and her nails raked feverishly along his back.

Their lovemaking had an intimacy it had not had before. This time they knew one another; and they had remembered more of each other than she would have expected.

She remembered the taste of his flesh and the pleasure of caressing it with her lips. She remembered how good it was to caress him and to feel his male response.

He had remembered how sensitive her nipples were, and how she had cried out in a mixture of denial and delight when his mouth had caressed the inside of her thigh.

He did it again now, less tentatively than last time, touching her so intimately and pleasurably that her body seemed to melt into a hot pool of delight. And all the time she could sense his own finely held control, his determination to give her pleasure before seeking any for himself, his care of her swollen body as though he feared to hurt either her or her child.

Such consideration touched her emotions in a way

that nothing else ever had. She wanted to reach out and embrace him, to cradle him against her, and tell him that she had lied and that her child was his, but even in the fierce, tumultuous throes of their flesh coming together, when Marcus's self-control splintered and he made love to her with a need that verged on the obsessional, she still managed to retain just enough sanity to hold back the words.

Her body imploded in silent ecstasy as she felt his shattering climax within her, his harsh cry of male triumph smothered against her mouth as he took it in a final, searing kiss. He eased her gently on to her side, and she touched the damp warmth of his chest with her fingertip, tracing the dark line of hair.

'It's getting light properly now,' she warned him.

'We'll just sleep for half an hour, and then I'll go. We have to talk about what happened just now, Diana. You know that, don't you?'

She must have betrayed more to him than she had thought. It would be hard now to deny to him that she wanted him . . . that she needed him.

Her eyelids dragged down as though they were tied to heavy weights. Marcus pulled her close to the warmth of his body and she curled up against him. The baby kicked and Marcus frowned as he felt the tiny fluttering movement.

For a moment he had almost forgotten that she was carrying another man's child. A man she still claimed to love. He really ought to leave. He would be late for milking, not to mention the potential gossip he was likely to cause by parking outside her house at this time of the morning, but the temptation to remain with her was too strong.

CHAPTER EIGHT

DIANA never knew quite what had woken her. She was only conscious of the change in the quality of the light filtering into the room. She looked towards the window and saw Marcus standing there.

He was fully dressed, and had obviously intended to leave without disturbing her. As she lay watching him she heard the church clock strike the hour. Seven—Marcus was going to be late for milking. She was just about to speak to him, when the sleep clouding her brain cleared and she became aware that his stance, even from behind, was clearly one of anger and disbelief.

A cold sensation of fear engulfed her as he turned round and she saw the photograph he was holding in his hand. On the window lay the letters from the solicitor, and it was obvious that he had been reading them.

'It was all a lie, wasn't it ... wasn't it?' he demanded fiercely. 'There is no Leslie ... no husband. You made him up. Why? Why, Diana? Why come here posing as a newly bereaved widow? What is it about you that makes you do such a thing?'

The shocked disgust in his eyes was like a knife being buried inside her. She had never imagined there could be pain like this, and it came to her in that moment that she loved him.

'Well? Are you going to tell me the truth?'

Suddenly, she felt bitterly angry. Her motives in acting the way she had had been for the protection of her child. *He* was the one who had been responsible for the growth of her deception. It had been because of *him* that she had been forced to lie and lie again.

'*Why* did you pretend you had a husband?'

And then as though in answer to his own question his eyes strayed to her body.

'My God.' His voice was hoarse with shock. 'If there was no husband then ... My child, Diana,' he said thickly. 'That's my child!'

He reached her in three strides, practically hauling her out of the bed, his fingers digging painfully into her upper arms.

'You lied to me. That's my child you're carrying, isn't it ... isn't it?'

'Yes.'

For what seemed like a long, long time there was silence between them. It stretched taut like wire, and it seemed to Diana's sensitive nerves that it stretched so tight that the very air around them was explosive with its tension.

'Right, I want to hear the whole story. The whole thing right from the beginning.'

'There isn't time now ... tonight ...' She was trying to buy time, trying to think what she should tell him.

'No, not tonight Diana, but now. If I leave it until tonight, what's to stop you running out on me? I want the truth. I think I have the right to demand it, don't you? My God!' he exploded bitterly. 'How could any woman do that to a man? Let him father her child and then keep it a secret. Why did you, why ...?

'I didn't. At least it wasn't like that. I didn't deliberately set out to get pregnant, Marcus. Leslie ...'

She saw him wince, and bit down hard on her bottom

lip to stop her self-control from fracturing into a thousand irreparable shards as he said savagely, 'Dear Christ, all this time I've been jealous of a shadow ... of a man who doesn't exist. You've been putting me through hell, do you know that? Have you *any* idea what it does to me to discover that Leslie is ...'

'Not is,' she told him bleakly. 'Was ... Leslie is dead ... she was my closest friend. She died of leukaemia. She was ill for a long, long time ... After her funeral I think I went a little bit crazy. That night ...'

She saw his eyes darken as though he was remembering something and he said hoarsely, 'You *were* a virgin, weren't you? Christ, didn't you even stop to think about what you were doing? About the risks you were running? Not just of pregnancy, but to your health?'

'Did you?'

She watched as the dark colour ran up under his skin. 'I wanted you too damn much to think of anything else,' he told her roughly.

'And of course, it's different for a man.'

'Not if he values his health,' Marcus contradicted her, surprising her. 'I told you at the time that I didn't go in for casual sex, if you remember.'

'And of course, Patty wasn't available. How disappointing for you. And how very frustrating. No wonder ...'

He shook her so hard that she was unable to complete her sentence. 'Don't you dare say that! I wasn't using you as a substitute for Patty. Good God, she's hardly more than a child.'

'Is that *really* how you see her? That wasn't the way she described your relationship to me,' she told him bitterly.

'Oh, Patty likes to exaggerate. She's very theatrical, but she and I have never been lovers, whatever she may have told you.' He made an exasperated sound deep in his throat. 'We're digressing. You still haven't told me why you lied to me about your pregnancy.'

'Isn't it obvious? I came here because I wanted a new start for myself and my child. I didn't want, and I still don't want, the stigma of illegitimacy hanging over him or her. I don't want to bring up my child in the anonymity of a large city. Leslie was a writer and she wrote a best seller, and she had made rather a lot of money. She willed it all to me.'

'*I* believe that a child deserves to have the love of both its parents,' Marcus told her bluntly.

'So do I, but not all children are fortunate enough to have that sort of family unit.'

'Ours can. I want you to marry me, Diana, just as soon as it can be arranged. In fact, I insist on it.'

'No.' She reacted instinctively against the panicky fear clawing through her. Talking about Leslie had reactivated all her old fears and dreads. She couldn't marry Marcus, she couldn't go through the trauma of losing someone she loved.

'Do you know what you're doing?' Marcus challenged. 'You're denying our child its right to a normal, happy family life. And you're doing so by the most arbitrary means I've ever seen.'

'Most men in your position would be only too delighted to be absolved from their responsibilities,' Diana flared.

'Maybe, but I'm not most men.'

'We can't marry,' Diana flung at him. 'We can't marry simply because ...'

'Between us we've started a new life. Can you think of any better reason?' he asked grimly. 'What are you going to tell our child when he or she asks why he doesn't have a father? Will you tell him the truth, Diana? That it's because you refused to marry me? Because if you don't I damn well will.'

'No... No... I won't let you come anywhere near my baby ...'

She tore herself away from him and scrambled off the bed, sick with terror as she raced for the door.

He mustn't know how much she wanted to give in and agree to what he was saying. She loved him and she wanted to marry him; she wanted them to share their child, but she was also frightened by the enormity of the commitment she would be making. She couldn't forget how it had felt to watch Leslie slowly slip away from her; the anguish of loving someone and losing them.

As she reached the door she wrenched it open. She heard Marcus call out something to her, but she was in too much of a panic to listen. She had forgotten the boxes piled at the top of the stairs and she stumbled into them and lost her balance.

The knowledge that she was going to fall down the stairs hit her almost before it happened. Like a film played in slow motion she was conscious of her body falling; of Marcus crying out her name; of pain and confusion, and then darkness.

She recovered consciousness briefly in the ambulance. Marcus was sitting beside her, his face white with shock and guilt, but it wasn't his fault, it was hers. She wanted to reach out and tell him so but it hurt too much to talk. She saw him look at her and saw the anguish in his eyes.

Her hand touched her stomach and she shuddered

suddenly. What if she lost her baby? She closed her eyes and prayed desperately, and then, like a child making a magic incantation against evil, she found herself promising that if only her baby was safe she would do whatever Marcus wanted. She would even marry him.

The vow hung in her mind as she fell back into unconsciousness, but she had made it and she clung to it like a good luck charm, almost as hard as she clung to Marcus's hand.

She was beginning to feel rather blasé about opening her eyes and finding herself in strange beds. This one had scratchy sheets, and felt uncomfortably hard.

'Good—so you've decided to rejoin us at last have you?'

She looked up into the face of the white-coated doctor bending over her.

'My baby . . .' She felt as though she were shouting, but in reality her voice was only a whisper. Her whole body ached, especially her back.

'My baby,' she pleaded again.

'Babies are tough little characters,' the doctor told her. 'Yours seems to be quite content where he is for the moment. We'll keep you under our eye for a couple of days though, just to be on the safe side.'

Diana closed her eyes and felt the hot tears come through her lids and down her face, as she sent up a prayer of thankfulness.

'Marcus . . .' She flushed brilliantly as she realised what she was saying, but the doctor seemed not to notice.

'Ah yes, that will be the gentleman pacing up and

down impatiently outside. You can see him, but only for a few minutes.'

She was in a small side ward, hers the only bed that was occupied. The doctor left.

Outside the sun had risen fully. The door opened and Marcus walked in.

'Now you really will be late for milking.'

She saw some of the strain leave his face when she spoke.

'Are you all right?' He came to her bedside, and stared anxiously down at her.

'Both of us are fine,' she assured him, watching the relief dawn in his eyes.

She felt so guilty. If anything had happened to their baby it would have been her fault for panicking so stupidly.

'God, when I think what could have happened!' His voice was a thick tortured sound that hurt her. She reached out and took his hand in hers.

'I feel the same way,' she told him huskily, 'but we were lucky, and nothing did happen.'

She looked directly into his eyes. 'I've changed my mind, Marcus. I'll marry you. I made a vow on the way here that if the baby was all right, I would.'

The delight that had been lightening his eyes faded abruptly, and she thought she must have mistaken it when he said slowly, 'I don't want you to rush into a decision.' He avoided looking at her as he walked over to the window and stared out. 'There are worse things a child can endure than an absent father. I was wrong to try and pressure you into marriage, Diana.' He turned round and looked directly at her. 'You don't have to marry me out of guilt, you know.'

What did he mean? Had he changed his mind? Was this why he was urging her to think over her decision? A wave of humiliated colour scorched her. She had been a fool. His initial offer of marriage had probably been nothing more than a chivalrous impulse which he had regretted almost the moment it was made.

No doubt he had been secretly relieved when she turned him down. It was obvious that she had stunned him with her *volte-face*.

Suddenly she felt dreadfully tired and depressed. The door opened and a nurse came in.

'Time's up for today, I'm afraid,' she said cheerfully. 'Our patient needs some sleep.'

It hurt that Marcus left without so much as the slightest protest. He was almost eager to leave, Diana thought wretchedly.

What on earth was the matter with her, anyway? Her emotions were sawing up and down like a yo-yo. One moment she was terrified at the very idea of commitment; the next she was close to tears because Marcus had changed his mind about marrying her. Why on earth couldn't she decide exactly what she did want?

She wanted Marcus. The knowledge whispered into her mind in much the same way that she had first realised she loved him. She wanted him to be part of her life; part of their child's life. She had been thrown into panic, as much by guilt as by fear. She had hated seeing the expression of incredulous disbelief in his eyes when he had realised who Leslie actually was, and how much she had lied to him. Her panic had been as much a defensive gesture as anything else, but it was too late to explain all that to him now.

In his eyes she must appear to be the most deceitful

person alive. She hadn't been able to explain to him how one small fib had led to bigger and bigger fabrications. She wanted to tell him the whole story, to explain to him about Leslie and how she had felt about her death, but now it was too late.

The nurse checking her pulse frowned. 'You really must try and relax,' she told her reprovingly. 'It isn't doing either you or your baby any good to get upset like this. You've had a very lucky escape, the pair of you.'

She slept through most of the morning, waking only when an orderly brought her lunch. From her window she could see visitors arriving, and she was suddenly struck by her own aloneness. When she had her baby would she be the only new mother in the ward with no family or friends around her?

Fresh tears welled in her eyes and she was just dashing them away when the door opened, and Ann came in carrying a large bunch of flowers and some fruit.

'You poor thing, Marcus told me what happened. I was coming in to see Ma anyway, so I thought I'd pop in and see how you were doing.'

'I'm all right, and Junior is being very patient with me.'

Ann smiled sympathetically. 'I *do* know how you feel. I very stupidly allowed myself to get high blood pressure with our first, and I was confined to hospital for the last few weeks. Worse than the waiting and the boredom, was the terrible feeling of guilt; the feeling that somehow I'd failed my baby. It doesn't last though. The moment I held John in my arms, I forgot that I was the most dreadful woman on earth, I was so proud of myself—and him.'

Diana couldn't help but laugh. Ann was as invigorating as a bracing wind.

'I can't stop long, but Ma did ask me to see if she could come and see you. They're keeping her in for another couple of days, and she's finding time hanging very heavily on her hands.'

Diana didn't know what explanation Marcus had given for her accident, but it was obvious that Ann did not know the truth. She would enjoy having Jane Simons' company, all the more so now that she had acknowledged to herself how much she loved her son.

'I'd love to see your mother,' she told Ann, 'but is she really well enough?'

'Don't worry, the nurses are keeping an eye on her.' She looked at her watch. 'I've got to go, otherwise I won't get back in time for the school run; it's my turn this week.'

The room seemed empty after she had gone. She felt restless and uncomfortable. Her bruised body ached, but it was the conflict that raged inside her that hurt the most.

Marcus had rejected her. She could hardly take it in. She didn't want to take it in, she admitted miserably.

The female doctor who came to check up on her frowned a little over her withdrawn misery, and counselled her reassuringly, 'Don't feel guilty about what happened; you'd be amazed the number of pregnant ladies who have falls. Babies are pretty tough creatures, you know; and agonising over what might have been won't do you any good at all.'

She wasn't to know that it wasn't the fall Diana was agonising over as much as Marcus's reaction to her acceptance of his proposal.

It had thrown her completely. She had become used to

him being there in her life; she had been spoiled by his numerous attempts to coax her into a relationship—as she had then thought, and it was only now that she realised how much she had come to count on him.

She had been deceiving herself. She couldn't live without human contact and love, and it was only now, when Marcus was lost to her, that she was able to accept how much he really meant to her.

Jane Simons came to see her later in the afternoon. It was a relief to see the older woman looking so well. Although she had forced herself to hide it at the time, Diana had been as appalled and frightened as Mrs Jenkins by that still figure sprawled on the ground.

'My dear, I've been hearing all about your fall. A similar thing happened to me when I was carrying Marcus. I felt so guilty. And then Ann ... but I suppose she's told you.' A warm smile lit Jane's face. 'Diana, I really came to thank you for all you did for me the other day. Mrs J is a treasure, but she's no use at all in an emergency. Of course, poor Marcus has been lashing himself into a fever of guilt about it, but I'm afraid the blame is really my own. I've struggled so hard to hang on to what little mobility and independence I do have, that I'm afraid I've overestimated my own capabilities.

'Marcus has been on at me for ages to have a companion. He's been frightened all along that something like this would happen. When my sister-in-law was alive it was different. She and I got on so well ... It's difficult explaining to Marcus how I feel when he's done so much for me already. Given up so much to ... Did you know that he was once engaged?'

Diana nodded.

'I never met the girl myself. She was an American,

and used to a far more sophisticated life-style than we have here. Marcus worked for her father. They were all set to get married, when my brother died and Marcus learned that he had inherited the farm. She expected him to sell up and invest the money with her father, and although Marcus has always denied it I can't help wondering—if it hadn't been for me, would he have done?'

Diana didn't know what to say to comfort her friend. 'Marcus doesn't strike me as a man who would let anyone else make his decisons for him,' she ventured at last.

'No ... no, he isn't. But he's like his father—a very compassionate and caring man, with a strong sense of duty. I can't get it out of my mind that he refused to sell the farm because of me ...'

'I'm sure that must have been part of it,' Diana admitted, knowing that the older woman wouldn't accept an easy lie. 'But he seems to love the farm, and he doesn't strike me as a man who's suffering from a broken heart.'

'No ... that's what Ann says. He does love the farm, but he's had a very hard job with it. My brother was old-fashioned in his methods, and he had let the breeding side of the farm go down. Marcus has had to work hard to boost that up again. It's only lately in fact that we've been making a profit on the breeding side of things. Perhaps I wouldn't feel so guilty if Marcus married. He's had several girlfriends, but none of them have ever been serious.'

'Not even Patty Dewar?'

Diana flushed guiltily, but it was too late to recall the question. Jane Simon looked surprised.

'Oh, I'm sure that Marcus looks on Patty as little more than a child. She's definitely not cut out to be a farmer's wife. No, Patty has her eyes set on stage-lights, I suspect.' She looked down at her lap and fiddled for a moment with her handkerchief.

'Diana, forgive me for interfering, but I suspect you know what I'm leading up to. Marcus has given up his own life for my sake once already, I don't want him to do it again. If he were to meet ... someone ... who for whatever reasons couldn't live on the farm, I would want him to sell it.

'I've talked to Ann about this, and with my share of the money from the farm I could have a small self-contained annexe built on to her house, and employ a companion-cum-nurse as Marcus has suggested.'

'Oh no, you mustn't do that!' Diana was horrified. 'Marcus would be so hurt.'

'But surely not as hurt as he would be if he lost the woman he loved. Diana my dear ... I'm not blind ... I've seen the way my son looks at you. And I've also noticed how determined you are to keep him at bay. If that's because of me ... or the farm ... It can be a lonely life for a young woman used to the bright lights of London.'

Diana was horrified. Good heavens! Did Jane really think that she ...

'Oh no ... please ... you mustn't think that.' Her eyes widened abruptly as she saw the pleased smile curving Jane's mouth. Her eyes twinkled naughtily as she watched the realisation dawn in Diana's eyes.

'I'm sorry, that was naughty of me, but you leapt to Marcus's defence so gallantly and determinedly that it was worth it. Diana, I know my son cares very deeply about you, and I'm sure you feel the same way about him. My dear, I know you must feel that it's too soon after your husband's death, and ...'

Diana shook her head pleadingly, unable to allow her to go on any longer.

'Please, I can't ...'

'I'm sorry.' Jane was instantly penitent. 'I had no right to interfere, but I love my son very much indeed, and I like you as well Diana. I shouldn't have tried to interfere.'

Diana bit her lip. 'You didn't ... it wasn't ... It isn't that I don't care about Marcus ...' was all she could manage.

Jane Simons patted her hand understandingly.

'It isn't the farm ... or you ... And anyway, I think Marcus has changed his mind.'

She heard Jane sigh. 'I can't believe that. Marcus isn't the kind of person who, having once made a commitment to someone, can go back on it.'

No, he wasn't, and what Diana feared now was that Marcus would come back to say that he would marry her, but for their child's sake, and not because he really wanted her. She didn't want that.

How ironic life could be—bitterly so at times.

CHAPTER NINE

THEY discharged her from hospital the next day. She went straight back to the pub, where Madge Davies greeted her with almost motherly concern.

Heaven alone knew what explanation Marcus had given for her accident, but it certainly couldn't have been the correct one. She guessed what it must have been a little later on, over a cup of welcome tea, when Madge said consolingly, 'You must have been terrified when you thought someone was trying to break in. After living in London I suppose you *do* think every sound outside is threatening, but of course it was only Marcus checking up that everything was all right because he had seen your light on.

'He said that it was the shock of him knocking on your door that made you fall, but luckily you'd forgotten to lock it and so he was able to get in. Still, you're all right now.'

Yes, she was, thank God.

They had told her to take things easy for a day or two at the hospital, but the house was now finished and she was anxious to move in. Her stock was already beginning to arrive, and her ad. for an assistant was in this week's newspaper; she had too much to do to waste time sitting around. Most of her furniture had now arrived, and the bookshelves were in place in the shop.

She moved into her new home midway through the week. Ann insisted on helping her, refusing to allow her to lift any of the heavy boxes.

The response to her ad. had been overwhelming. She had sifted through the replies, and was going to interview half a dozen of the applicants.

She was going to have a very busy summer, she reflected wryly as she closed her back door after her helpers. First there was the launch party for the bookshop, then the summer fête, and then, before she knew where she was, it would be November and the birth of her baby would be imminent.

Feeling restless, despite her tiring day, she went back downstairs after she had eaten and started sorting out some of the new books.

Choosing her stock had been one of the hardest decisions she had had to make, and she only hoped she had chosen well. A large part of her space would, of necessity, be devoted to paperbacks; she was still considering branching out into cards and wrapping paper, and a chance comment by a member of the fête committee had set her thinking in another direction.

The other woman had remarked how difficult it was for the local amateur artists' group to get hold of paints and other equipment. The nearest shop stocking what they needed was in Gloucester, and Diana was mentally debating whether she could afford to turn any of her selling space over to artists' requirements.

The summer fête was less than a month away now, midway through September—late for a summer fête really, but Ann had explained that it also embraced their harvest festival.

She had scheduled her opening launch party for the first weekend in September, and at Ann's suggestion had approached the Mothers' Union and the Women's

Guild about catering for the affair.

'They really are good,' Ann had told her, 'and they would be glad of the opportunity to make some money— for the restoration of the church roof. We're more than half-way towards our target, and every little helps.'

Her baby was due at the end of November, although she had been warned that as it was a first baby it might be late. She was now in her sixth month, and apart from the shock of her fall she had never felt healthier.

The books she had unpacked belonged on the top shelves of the new bookcases. The sudden surge of restless energy that had overtaken her had not abated, and she looked round impatiently for the lightweight aluminium step-ladder she had bought specially for the shop.

She found them after some searching, tucked away in a corner of the store-room, and carried them through to the shop. The books she had unpacked were mainly dictionaries and other reference volumes.

Holding a pile of them, she mounted the step-ladder, and started to stack them on the shelves.

If she did marry Marcus she would have to give all this up ... She was surpised how little she minded. The living accommodation was self-contained and could be let out, and she would always find someone to manage the shop for her.

As Marcus's wife she would be needed at the farm. She felt a small curl of pleasure build up inside her as she abandoned herself to the fantasy of imagining what marriage to Marcus would be like, coming abruptly down to earth when she remembered his response to her acceptance of his proposal.

How ironic it was that after resisting any sort of

relationship at all with him, the moment she admitted to herself that she was wrong and that loving and needing him were more important than the pain she risked in those emotions, he should be the one to step back from her.

Her euphoria left her, despair taking its place. She had been right to fear loving him, she thought miserably as she completed her task and climbed down from the ladder.

The evening stretched emptily ahead of her. What was Marcus doing? His mother was back now, perhaps they were having dinner together, or more likely Marcus would be out somewhere on the farm working.

The phone rang and she rushed to answer it, but it was only Ann asking if she would like to have lunch with them on Sunday. She wanted to say 'yes' but Marcus would probably be there, and the ball was in his court now. The last thing she wanted was for him to think she was trying to push him into marriage—or anything else; so she refused.

Moping wasn't going to do her the slightest bit of good, she told herself firmly. There was any amount of things she ought to be doing, and work would help to take her mind off Marcus.

She worked all evening but she didn't stop thinking about him, and when she went to bed all she could remember was how they had made love here in her bed, and then how he had turned on her afterwards, after he had realised the truth. She supposed that it had been rather stupid to give her fictitious husband the same name as her dead friend, but she had panicked when she realised that Marcus was going to be living so close to her, and Leslie's had been the first name that came to mind.

The rest in hospital must have done her good, she decided two days later, on her way back from a check-up which had laid any lingering doubts at rest. Both she and the baby were perfectly healthy, and, as an extra bonus, she was riding on the crest of a wave of energy that was permitting her to get through much more work than she had envisaged.

As she drove she glanced at her watch. She had less than an hour before her first interview of the afternoon. All in all she had six girls to see. She had worked with younger girls under her control at the TV station, and had no qualms about employing someone.

She got back with half an hour to spare, and remembering the doctor's warning that she could still do with a little more weight she made herself a salad lunch.

She had just cleared away the plates, when she heard the doorbell to the shop. Her first applicant was a rather shy girl of eighteen, with a long mane of untidy hair, and frightened blue eyes. Diana put her at her ease and started to interview her.

It was almost six o'clock before she showed the last applicant out. She went back inside and studied the notes she had taken. She had already made her decision, but she just wanted to make doubly sure.

At seven o'clock she stood up and stretched. Yes, she had been right. The girl who had made the best impression on her had been perhaps a trifle off-putting to look at with her wild post-punk hair-do, and garishly coloured clothes. But her answers to Diana's questions had been intelligent ones; she was the eldest of a family of four, and therefore accustomed to dealing with children. She had managed to add up the columns of figures Diana had given her, accurately and without access to a calculator. She had also worked in a shop before, although only as a Saturday girl, and Diana felt that she would be able to teach her how to handle some of the paperwork involved in running the shop.

She nibbled the end of her pen and looked down at the names she had written on the paper.

Mary White had been the first girl she had interviewed. Too shy and withdrawn to handle full-time responsibility for the shop, but Diana had nevertheless sensed potential in the girl. With a little encouragement ... She gnawed the pen again and then came to a decision. She would offer Mary a job as a part-time assistant—there would be times, like Christmas, she hoped, when she would need two girls.

She pulled out her small portable typewriter and started to work.

Ann's suggestion that she approach the Women's Guild and Mothers' Union concerning buffet food for her launch party had proved a good one. Given a generous budget both groups came up with a menu that sounded mouth-watering. Diana had stipulated quality rather than quantity, and she was highly delighted with the imaginative suggestions submitted.

She was keeping her fingers crossed that the weather would stay fine and that her guests would be able to go outside into the garden.

The boys' hard work had revealed the makings of two very attractive cottage garden borders of perennial plants—some of which had gone to seed, but which Ann had advised her could quite easily be replaced. With the benefit of Ann's advice, and her recommendation of a garden centre not very far out of town, Diana had high hopes that in a week's time, when she held her launch party, the garden would look as attractive as the shop and her home.

Not even to herself would she admit that all this frantic activity was designed, at least in part, to keep her mind off Marcus. Since her acceptance of his proposal and her return from hospital, she hadn't seen or heard from him; the classic case of a man having cold feet, she told herself, wryly. The problem was that she had tended to put Marcus up on a pedestal, without even being aware of it. He was so popular locally, and so well thought of, that she had made the mistake of investing him with all manner of virtues and qualities that only a perfect human being would possess.

He had offered to marry her in a fit of gallantry, and once he had had time to think about the consequences of his proposal he had had second thoughts—how could she blame him for being reluctant to take on the commitment of her and their child when she herself had fought desperately to evade any sort of commitment to any human being herself?

It was irrational of her to be so despairingly hurt by his rejection—but she was. She loved him. She realised it now, and she could only marvel that she had been able to deceive herself for so long.

Her invitations for the launch had already been sent out, and, of course, she had invited Ann and her husband, and Jane Simons. It was stupid to feel as excited as a young girl contemplating her first date, she told herself when she woke up on the morning of the launch party. After all, the situation being what it was,

Marcus was all too likely not to come.

Both her new employees were joining in on the launch party. She had decided that it was a good way to break the ice, and to see how they reacted to the business.

In addition to some of her suppliers, and new friends in the locality, she had also invited one or two people from the TV station, plus several other members of the media world. You never knew, it might get her a little bit of extra publicity.

The new dress she had worn to dinner at Ann's was ideally suited to the warm late summer afternoon. The Mothers' Union and the Guild, true to their promises, arrived in the middle of the morning, complete with trestle tables, plates, glasses and cutlery.

Diana could only marvel at their efficiency as they set to work, and when she said as much to one of them, the woman smiled appreciatively. 'Oh, we're loving every minute of this,' she told Diana. 'It isn't often we get the chance to cater for an occasion where keeping the cost down isn't the prime concern. You'd be surprised how inventive one learns to be with potted beef sandwiches and Victoria sponges.'

The first of her guests started arriving at two-thirty; by half past three, the shop was full, and the overspill reached out into the garden.

Too busy in her role as hostess to linger too long with any one group, Diana kept hearing snatches of conversation, sometimes technical and barely comprehensible, between two of her major suppliers, who were talking about profit margins and the relative merits of printing in various countries; and at others, far more homely, as when she heard a group of mothers discussing the problem of steering children away from TV and into avenues that exercised their own imaginations.

Her mural occasioned a great deal of admiration and interest; the photographer from the local paper bemoaned the fact that they wouldn't be able to feature it in colour, and a friend of a friend, brought along at the last moment, turned out to be a journalist on one of the Sunday supplements, who was interested in doing a feature on her for his magazine.

'Quite a change from busy career woman working for a TV station to living in a small country town running a bookshop. A lot of our readers are really into this "back to the simple life" stuff now, and an article on you should go down very well.'

They discussed it for several minutes, and then out of the corner of her eye Diana saw that Ann and Michael had arrived.

Her heart sank when she realised that Jane Simons was with them. That must mean that Marcus wasn't coming. This was what she had dreaded, and her spirits plunged instantly. She had both looked forward to and dreaded seeing him all week, and now he wasn't coming. She excused herself to the journalist and went forward to greet the late arrivals.

'Sorry about this,' Ann apologised, kissing her, 'but Michael had an emergency and we were all delayed.'

'Marcus sends his apologies too,' Jane Simons put in. 'They're working desperately hard to get the last of the long meadow cleared of hay.'

A plausible excuse, but Diana wasn't deceived. Marcus would have been here if he had wanted to come.

As yet, Jane hadn't seen the mural, and she exclaimed over it with real pleasure.

'I'm thinking of having something similar done in the

nursery, but not yet,' Diana told her.

'All's obviously well in that direction. You look positively blooming, conventional though it sounds to say so.'

'As you do,' Diana told her. 'I must admit I was terrified when you had your fall. It's so frightening to see someone lying there unconscious and not being able to help them.'

'Yes, I feel so guilty about it. It was all my own fault, and Marcus has started fussing like a mother hen. Mrs J barely lets me out of her sight, and it's tiring her out, poor soul, not to mention what it's doing to my temper, I'm afraid. I'm more worried about Marcus than I am about myself.'

Ann and Michael had wandered off, and Jane Simons glanced shrewdly at Diana before she went on.

'I don't know what's happened between my son and you, Diana, but I do know that it's making him very withdrawn. I know I've brought this subject up with you before, but if it's the farm ...'

'No ... No, it isn't that.' Diana shook her head decisively.

'Then what is it?' Jane asked gently. 'Or can't you tell me?'

For one awful moment, Diana thought she was about to burst into tears. She was behaving like a child herself, she derided herself.

'I know you must still grieve for your husband,' Jane continued, 'but ...'

Diana couldn't let her go on.

'It ... it isn't that ...' she gulped miserably. 'Jane, I can't talk to you about it, but please believe me, there's nothing ... There's nothing I want more than to have

Marcus's love,' she admitted bravely. 'Marcus is the one with the doubts,' she went on quietly, reaching out to touch Jane pleadingly on her arm, as she begged, 'please, don't tell him that we've had this conversation. I should hate him to think I'm trying to pressure him into anything ...'

'Don't worry. I won't say a word,' Jane assured her. 'I had no right to ask you such a question in the first place, and I'm touched that you felt able to confide your feelings to me, Diana. You know,' she added gravely, 'that I've become very fond of you, don't you? And I can't deny that I'd love to have you as my daughter-in-law. I was so pleased when I thought Marcus had fallen for you, and then I was worried because you seemed to be rejecting him, but if you ever need to talk to anyone, Diana, regardless of the fact that I'm Marcus's mother, please come to me, won't you? Your own family must seem dreadfully far away at times. I think, perhaps because none of us knew him, we all tend to forget what you've been through in losing your husband.'

Diana couldn't endure any more. She excused herself hurriedly, spotting a colleague from her TV days heading towards her, toting a glass of wine and balancing a plate of goodies.

'Fab food,' she commented, consuming a morsel of smoked salmon greedily. 'Lovely place as well—almost too quaint and olde worlde—but what's all this I hear about you being a widow, and a prospective mother to boot? You kept it all very quiet when you were at work!'

Mercifully, the other woman didn't seem to realise that there never had been a husband, merely believing that Diana hadn't mentioned him.

'Oh, you know how it is ...' she shrugged dismissively, and heaved a soft sigh of relief when someone else came up to join them and the subject was dropped.

She had realised she was taking a risk in inviting people down here who knew her from her old life, but she had been so miserable since realising how much she loved Marcus that the dangers had barely impinged upon her.

No sooner had her old colleague gravitated back to the buffet, than Madge Davies cornered her.

'This food is out of this world,' she commented enviously. 'Perhaps I ought to get the ladies of the parish into the pub to exercise their skills there.'

'Maybe you should,' Diana agreed. 'Apparently they're always looking for ways to add to the church restoration fund—you've got enough land at the back of your place to stage weekend barbecues at lunch-times. You could get them to cater for you. I'm sure they would.'

'That's a great idea!' Looking excited and thoughtful, Madge hurried off.

Everyone seemed to be enjoying themselves apart from her, Diana thought wryly. Even her two new employees were happily mingling with the general throng.

Susie's punk hair-do had been tamed down somewhat, she noticed, and Mary's shyness seemed to have eased slightly too.

At five o'clock, people started to drift away.

Ann, Michael and Jane were the very last to leave, after six o'clock, and it seemed to Diana that Jane in particular was anxious about something.

She ought not to have confided in her, Diana thought

guiltily. It was bound to make her feel awkward and embarrassed.

'We've got to go,' Michael said at last. 'Evening surgery starts soon.'

Her two new employees stayed behind to help clear up. The Mothers' Union, who had supplied the china, cutlery and glasses, had told Diana not to bother washing anything, but simply to leave it and they would be round for it in the morning; but her new kitchen had a dishwasher, and it seemed just as easy to run everything through it and then pack it away, especially with Susie and Mary to help her.

The tablecloths she bundled into a plastic bin liner ready for the laundry, and between them the two girls managed to unfasten and stack away the trestle tables.

'Marvellous,' Diana approved, when Susie straightened up from vacuuming the carpet. 'You've both done wonders.' She unlocked her desk to remove the two envelopes she had prepared beforehand.

'Since you aren't officially employed yet, this is a small payment for today's services.'

'You're paying us?' Mary's eyes widened with surprised delight. 'But it wasn't like work, it was fun.'

'Yeah, it was real cool,' Susie agreed.

After they had gone, Diana suffered the gloomy effects of post-party let down. She wandered from room to room, hating the emptiness of the house. Her restless energy took her out into the garden. The greenhouse frame still needed a new coat of paint. She would do it now, she decided impulsively; anything to stop her from thinking about Marcus. Right up until the end of the party she had gone on hoping that he would appear; right up until his family left, she had gone on believing that he might relent.

A thought struck her. Was this his way of telling her that he didn't want to marry her? Tears blinded her for a moment as she went to collect her step-ladder, and she brushed them away with an impatient hand. What was the point in crying? Tears wouldn't bring him back.

She was half-way along one side of the greenhouse when she began to be aware of the nagging pain in her back. She straightened up, rubbing the tender spot, and stretching. Beneath her the steps wobbled slightly, and then suddenly she was snatched off them, and swung hard against a warm male chest.

'For Christ's sake, will you never learn! What the devil were you trying to do? I thought you *wanted* this child.'

Marcus ... Marcus had come after all! She was too overjoyed to register the grim fury in his voice, too deliriously happy to do anything other than close her eyes and burrow closer to the male warmth of him; glorying in the sensation of his body against her own, his arms holding her close, his voice shivering in her ear.

'Diana ... Look at me.'

Reluctantly she opened her eyes, wincing when she saw the fury in his. 'Just what were you trying to do?' he demanded again.

Her small bubble of happiness burst.

'I wasn't *trying* to do anything,' she told him flatly. 'I was simply painting.'

'Oh, you were simply painting, were you?'

She could feel the anger vibrating his chest. 'Forgive me, but, as I understood it, the doctors specifically warned you to take things easy. Didn't you hear them, Diana, or are you tired of carrying my child?' he demanded emotively. 'Are you ...'

Ashen-faced Diana pulled away from him. 'No ...' Dear God, how could he think that of her! Her revulsion showed in her face, and instantly his own expression changed.

'I'm sorry,' he apologised contritely. 'It was just seeing you there ... after that last time.'

They were standing apart now and much as she longed to move back into his arms, Diana lacked the courage to make the first move. She ran her tongue over her dry lips. Why had he come to see her? Had he made up his mind? Was he ...?

'I thought my mother would be here,' he told her, shattering all her hopes.

'She was, but she left half an hour ago with Ann and Michael.'

'Oh, she said she'd wait for me, but it took us longer than we expected to clear the field.' His forehead creased, and Diana was immediately conscious of the grim tiredness about him that she hadn't noticed before. He was wearing faded but clean jeans and an equally faded shirt. He must have stopped to shower before coming out, because she could still smell the soap clinging to his skin. It made her want to nuzzle closer to him and absorb the scent of him.

Closing her eyes against the prickle of tears stinging them she swayed slightly.

Instantly his hands bit into her arms. 'Why ... why did you change your mind about marrying me, Diana?'

The harshness in his voice cut into her. She opened her eyes, and saw that his were dark with anger mixed with other more complicated emotions. She shivered. If she hadn't looked at him she could almost have thought she heard pain in his voice.

'What do you want to know for? You don't want to marry me now, anyway.'

'But you want to marry me, apparently. Why? You were so determined that you didn't want me.'

'I've already told you why.' She couldn't bear much more of this. If he kept on questioning her, hurting her, she would start telling him the truth—that she loved him.

'Oh yes, so you have,' he agreed cynically. 'But *were* you telling me the truth? You've told me so many lies, haven't you?' he asked bitterly. 'There were so many evasions . . . so much deceit. I was so wrong about you, wasn't I? I thought you were just guilty about making love with me—about wanting me—so soon after your husband's death. I bent over backwards making allowances for you, Diana, telling myself that you needed time, that I mustn't rush you; but all the time you were simply playing a game—that's all it ever was to you, wasn't it?'

She could see the fury glittering in his eyes; sense it building up inside him, but she simply bowed her head, knowing she had no valid means of defence.

'God, how you must have laughed at me behind my back! How amusing you must have found my "understanding" of your grief.' His mouth twisted bitterly.

'No!' The cry was torn from deep within her. 'No . . . you don't understand, it wasn't like that!'

'Then just what the hell was it like?' he demanded savagely, reaching for her, and practically shaking her. 'Because I sure as hell am driving myself insane trying to understand what it is that makes you tick, lady.

'Oh, God!' He released her abruptly with a grimace of

distaste. 'What the hell are you doing to me? You incite me to violence, do you know that? If I don't leave now, I won't be responsible for what I might do to you. When I think of how you deliberately let me think ... let me sympathise ... Oh, God!'

The tortured curse was drawn from deep in his throat, leaving her own raw and aching. Much as she longed to comfort him, to restore his faith in her, Diana knew that there was nothing she could say.

She stood like a statue watching him go, unaware of the river of tears that slid silently down her face.

That was it then; there wasn't going to be any marriage; any happy-ever-afters where they would share their lives and their child. Thank God she had managed to stop herself from telling him that she loved him. That would have been the final humiliation.

She walked slowly back to the house, her surge of energy depleted, leaving her weak and shaky. Upstairs in her bedroom, she shivered even though she wasn't really cold. Only Marcus's arms could warm her and disperse this cold lump of misery inside her, only Marcus could bring warmth and light back into her life.

CHAPTER TEN

SHE told herself that she had a child to live for; that she owed it to Leslie, and her baby, to pull herself together. She was, after all, no worse off than she had been when she first came here, and then she had been so happy, so full of plans.

Now all those plans seemed unimportant. She had excused herself from any more work for the fête on the grounds that she wasn't feeling very well. She had barely noticed the concerned look Ann gave her. She was withdrawing into herself like a tortoise into its shell, and she wasn't going to let anything draw her out again.

She spent long hours simply sitting and staring into space. Her energy had gone, and in its place was a lassitude that took the colour from her cheeks, and left her without any appetite, tired-looking and visibly drawn.

Both Mary and Susie commented on it. Susie, beneath the outlandish clothes and peacock hair colour, was a motherly soul, and at any other time Diana would have been amused by her attempts to get her to eat. In the small kitchenette behind the stock-room, Susie cooked scrambled eggs, and brought her a plateful, or offered her pizza, or home-made cake she had brought from home.

At the back of her mind a tiny voice told her that she was being childish; that she was deliberately trying to punish herself for the lies she had told, and that in doing so she was risking both her own health and that of her child. At last, unable to bear her pain any longer, she told Susie that she was going up to London for the day. She was aware of the younger girl's concerned look, but she refused to acknowledge it.

The train journey seemed to take for ever. London overwhelmed her with its noise and dirt. She walked aimlessly along once familiar streets, before taking a taxi to her ultimate destination.

Now in the last flush of summer, the cemetery blossomed with flowers and trees. She wasn't the only visitor, and she paused once, to watch a gnarled old man unsteadily putting some flowers into a vase. He was crying, and Diana felt her own tears start up in sympathy.

She walked slowly towards Leslie's grave. The tombstone was new-looking and stark, but her rosemary had started to grow. She would bring her child here one day, and tell her the story of how he or she came to be conceived.

Now, when her child asked if she had loved its father she would be able to reply honestly that she had—loved him and lost him.

She put her head down against the cool stone and felt the slow remorselesss slide of tears down her cheeks. No matter how much she cried it did nothing to ease the pain inside her. She heard someone walking along the path, but she didn't move. Scenes of grief were so familiar here that no one felt any need to comment on them or interfere.

The footsteps stopped, a shadow blotting out the warmth of the sun. She moved her head and turned round, suddenly conscious of how remote the cemetery was, how vulnerable her own position. Fear chilled down her spine, and she struggled to stand up.

Instantly, a male hand came out to help her. The sun was dazzling her; she shaded her eyes, and felt as though the earth was dropping away from her, as she saw Marcus standing there.

'It's all right, Diana. It's all right now.'

Unbelievably, he was holding her, cradling her as though she was a child, and she was letting him, letting the grief and the guilt pour out with her wrenching sobs.

How long they stood like that she didn't know. All she knew was that, unbelievably, Marcus was with her, holding her as she had longed for him to do, stroking her hair and whispering soft words of comfort. She raised her tear-wet face to him.

'How ... how did you know where I was?'

A grave smile touched his mouth, softening its hard outline. 'I remembered you saying once that you'd been here. I contacted your solicitor and asked him for the address. Ann called to see you at the shop, and Susie told her how concerned about you she was. Between them, my mother and my sister have reduced me to the state of the lowest of the low, believe me,' he told her with a grimace, adding so quietly that at first she thought she had misheard, 'My mother says you love me, is that true?'

He must have seen the shock and indecision in her eyes, because he took both her hands in his and held her firmly.

'No evasion ... no prevarication. Trust me just this once, Diana, and tell me the truth.'

'Yes ... Yes I do.'

With her admission she felt the weight of her guilt

slide from her heart. No matter what happened now, he would at least know that she had cared about him, that their child did matter to her.

She swallowed hard and looked at him, unable at first to bear to do so until he cupped her face with one hand and tilted it up to meet his eyes.

The look of love and passion blazing out of them burned through her. 'I never thought I'd hear you say that to me.' His voice shook with emotion. 'I love you so much . . . right from that first moment . . . right from the very first time I touched you.'

'But the last time we met . . . you were so angry——' She shivered, and he touched her comfortingly.

'We'll talk about that later, right now I want you to know that I'm sorry for what I said to you, but I was out of my mind with pain. I wanted to marry you because I couldn't bear to live without you, and there you were telling me that you were willing to marry me because of a vow made in a moment of intense fear. Have you any idea of how that made me feel? I was so obviously unimportant to you . . . I . . .' He shook his head, his voice suspended by the intensity of his feelings. 'Marry me, Diana. Come and live with me and . . .'

'Be your love?' she finished for him. 'Gladly—gladly my darling, dearest Marcus.' She flung herself into his arms, and kissed him with all the pent-up passion of her feelings.

Beneath her mouth she felt the shock and then the response of his, and then he was the one kissing her, his hands hot and urgent on her body, his small cry of frustration as he pushed her away a soothing balm to her own aroused desire.

'I can't make love to you here,' he told her thickly. 'In

fact, I suspect I'm not going to be able to make love to you anywhere until we're respectably married. I can get a special licence. How about it, my love? Are you brave enough to commit yourself to me so quickly, say, in three days' time?'

What was there to be brave about? And as for commitment . . . hadn't she given him that the first time she gave him her body?

'Three days!' she teased. 'Will it really take as long as that?'

'It won't all be plain sailing,' Marcus told her as he drove her home. 'There's bound to be some gossip.'

'And we'll have to tell your mother and Ann the truth,' Diana put in. 'I know she'd love my baby anyway, but I do want your mother to know that he or she is your child as well.'

'Everything you say makes me love you more, do you know that?' Marcus told her thickly, narrowly avoiding an affronted pedestrian as he leaned across to kiss her.

They were married three days later, very quietly, in London, without telling anyone. Marcus had booked them into the hotel where it had all started. Diana laughed when she saw their room number. 'I asked for it specially,' Marcus told her.

From their hotel room, Marcus rang his mother, Diana curled possessively against his side, his hand supporting and gently caressing the swollen weight of her breast.

'You're what? Married? Oh, my dears . . .' He held the phone away from his ear so that Diana could hear his mother's pleased response.

'We're having the shortest honeymoon on record and should be back late tomorrow evening,' he went on.

'She wants to have a word with you.' He handed Diana the receiver.

'Diana, my dear, I'm so pleased. I told you that he loved you, didn't I? You and your child are both very welcome in our family.'

Diana took a deep breath. There was no easy way of doing this.

'*Our* child,' she corrected shakily. 'Marcus is the father of my baby . . . it's a long story, and one I promise I'll tell you, but I just wanted you to know.'

For a moment there was silence, and she wished passionately that she had kept the truth to herself until she could tell Jane face to face, but her opening had seemed so opportune that she hadn't been able to stop herself from using it.

'My dear . . .' There was a wealth of compassion and understanding in Jane Simons' husky words. 'I can't tell you how pleased that makes me.'

Diana handed the receiver back to her new husband. 'I've told her,' she said, unnecessarily.

'I do hope you realise the significance of this room,' Marcus commented half an hour later, after the waiter had arrived with their supper, and left an ice-bucket with champagne.

Diana gave him an impish grin, and said cheekily, patting her stomach. 'Well, if I don't, there's something here that's sure to remind me.'

'We haven't talked about Leslie properly yet, have we?' Marcus said softly. 'I haven't told you yet that I *do* understand what made you act the way you did. I suppose it was just the shock of discovering that you'd been using a fictitious husband to keep me at bay that made me so furious and unreasonable. You see, I'd been so jealous of him, so bitterly resentful of the fact that you were carrying his child and not mine, that you weren't the woman of my fantasies, created only for me and me alone, but another man's wife.'

'I didn't lie because of you ... at least not in the sense you meant,' Diana told him, swallowing the lump of emotion his words brought to her throat. 'Once I knew I was pregnant, I decided it was an omen, a sign that I should make a completely new life for myself. I never dreamed we'd meet again, so I made up a fictitious husband for our baby ... I didn't want him or her growing up under any slur of illegitimacy, and it made things so much easier for me as well. By the time we met, I'd already established myself as a widow and it was too late to go back. I was terrified you would discover the truth, and that it was your child. I don't know why ... Leslie's long illness and her death made me view any kind of emotional or physical commitment in a very distorted way. I suppose what happened to her gave me a terrible dread of something similar happening to someone else that I loved.'

'Yes, I can imagine how terrible it must be to see a young life destroyed so cruelly,' Marcus agreed sombrely. 'It was bad enough for us with Ma ... seeing her freedom curtailed, seeing her always confined to her wheelchair. It's odd, isn't it, how we suffer more for others in that way than we do for ourselves.'

'Leslie was dreadfully depressed at times. She used to beg me to help her to end ... things.'

'Ma had her depressions too,' Marcus told her

heavily. 'When she had her fall.'

Diana covered his hand with hers and felt it tremble.

'I'll always be grateful to her for telling me that you loved me,' he said, 'otherwise God knows how much more time we might have wasted. I couldn't believe it . . . but I wanted to believe it so much.'

'All I could think about was how much you must despise me for all the lies I'd told. Everything you said seemed to confirm it.'

'That was just sheer frustrated rage. I suppose it hurt my pride that you'd deceived me so completely. But what hurt most of all was the knowledge that you had been prepared to keep from me the fact that you were carrying my child.'

'Because I thought it was the right thing to do. Can you forgive me?'

He took her hand and pressed a kiss into its soft palm. 'There's nothing to forgive.

Later that night, wrapped in each other's arms in the lazy aftermath of love, Marcus said dreamily, 'I thought at the time that the woman I made love to in this hotel bedroom was someone very special. Now I know exactly how special, special is,' he added appreciatively, laughing as he felt her embarrassed wriggle.

'For a pregnant lady, Mrs Simons, you're amazingly provocative and sexy, do you know that?'

'I don't think the blame for that lies entirely with me, *Mr* Simons,' she taunted him back.

'Ah, well, you know what they say about abstinence,' Marcus responded, running his hands appreciatively over her body, and pulling her close to him.

'I thought that was absence,' Diana commented

muzzily, but it was really too much of an effort to talk, and far to much of a waste of time when her lips would far rather be doing other things than forming senseless words. Things like adoring the unique flavour and texture of Marcus's skin. Things like tasting and tantalising the male body so close to her own, as she was being teased and tantalised in turn.

Marcus's hands and then his lips moved in tender exploration over her throat and then her breasts. She gasped his name and drew him closer, eager again for the awesome sensation of having him within her. They made love gently but fulfillingly, falling asleep to make love again in the pale grey light of the false dawn.

'That was some honeymoon, Mrs Simons,' Marcus teased her later as they drove out of London on their homeward journey.

It was good to hear him joke; good to share that light-heartedness. Her fears and doubts had gone, dispersing like mist in the heat of the sun. Now she could see them in context for what they were; the perfectly natural reaction of any human being to the loss, through a long, despairing illness, of someone they loved. It was like emerging from a long dark tunnel into the light.

Four weeks later, standing in the kitchen of Whitegates, she and Marcus were on the verge of having their first marital quarrel.

'No,' Marcus said positively. 'Look, I *do* understand your feelings, Di, but this is our first baby. For both your sakes I want you to be safely installed in hospital when the time comes.'

'But Marcus, both your mother and her mother before her had their children—*all* their children, here at the farm, and I want to do the same,' Diana protested stubbornly.

They had been arguing about this since last night when she had announced that she had been giving serious consideration to the idea of a home birth.

She had already gone into it at some length with the local maternity unit, and after some enthusiastic persuasion, both from the midwife and from Diana herself, Dr Thomas had agreed that he could see no reason—if her pregnancy continued as trouble-free as it was at present—why she should not give birth at home.

'Look, Diana, this isn't something I'm prepared to argue with you about,' Marcus told her grimly. 'I happen to think that the best place for both you and our child is a hospital, with all the modern technology at hand if . . . if it should be needed.'

Diana couldn't budge him, as she commented to her mother-in-law later that afternoon. 'It's been like arguing with a combine harvester—I feel as though I've been shredded, threshed, and turned out in a nicely tied-up package,' she grumbled. 'He doesn't seem to appreciate that there's more to having a baby than modern technology.'

'Well, I *can* see his point,' Jane Simons demurred, 'but I can also see yours, Diana. My husband was just the same, you know. He was determined Marcus would be born in Hereford.'

'But he wasn't, was he?' Diana commented with a grin. 'How did you manage it?'

'Nature managed it for me . . . that's how.'

'Well, perhaps she'll be very generous and manage it for me as well,' Diana commented wryly.

* * *

Apart from Marcus's stubbornness over her desire to have her baby at home, Diana had never been happier. They made love every night, not as passionately perhaps as they both would have liked, but there was something unique and very special about the tenderness of the way Marcus held her; about his care of her and their child.

She was into her eighth month now and beginning to feel uncomfortable. Picking things up from the floor was almost an impossibility, and she needed Marcus's help to get into and out of the bath.

Initially, after their marriage, Jane Simons had told them both that they need not worry that she would intrude into their privacy, but Diana had told her immediately, that the boot was very much on the other foot.

'With Marcus so busy on the farm, I'd be lonely here without you,' she told the other woman firmly and warmly, and so they had got into the habit of sharing their afternoons and having dinner together when Marcus came in.

In the evening, if he wasn't out working, Diana helped him with his office work. Two days a week she drove into town to check on Susie's management of the shop. Mary now worked there full-time as well, and between them both girls were making an excellent job of it. After Christmas she intended to see if she could find a tenant for the living quarters upstairs.

She and Jane also had big plans to redecorate the farm, but like everything else, these would have to wait until after the birth of the baby.

Upstairs, in a room off their own, the nursery was being prepared. In a shop in Hereford, the cot and pram and the rest of their equipment had been chosen, to be delivered in time for the baby's arrival.

Summer had given way to autumn, with clear crisp days and fresh sharp scents in the air.

Marcus's cowman was predicting an early winter, and sure enough, late in October they woke up to a hard frost, and by the end of that week the distant Welsh mountains had their first powdering of snow.

In November, the temperature dropped sharply, and there were fresh falls of snow in the hills.

In the middle of the month, Diana began to feel tired and tetchy. However she sat or lay she felt uncomfortable, and a visit to the GP confirmed that her baby was ready to be born.

The hard frosts had delayed the autumn ploughing, and when she got back Marcus was out somewhere on the farm.

When Marcus eventually did come in, looking tired and drawn, she decided to keep Dr Thomas's warning that her baby was likely to be early rather than late to herself.

Ann and Michael were coming round for dinner, and Diana urged him upstairs to shower and change.

'No chance of you coming with me, I suppose?' he asked with a grin, surveying her newly made-up face, and the fluid lines of her one and only remaining fitting party dress.

'None at all,' Diana confirmed with an answering smile. 'I can hear a car, I think Ann and Michael have arrived.'

'My sister always did have excellent timing,' Marcus grumbled, disappearing in the direction of the stairs.

Later, Jane was inclined to blame the heavy meal; Ann opined that it was her visit to the hospital and subsequent examination that was responsible; while Diana merely said placidly that it was neither, it was simply that Mother Nature had decided for herself that the time was right.

Whatever the cause, the pangs of discomfort she had suffered on the way home worsened throughout the meal, combined with another and more insidious ache that gradually spread in waves that surged and then receded, quietly and occasionally at first, with increasing urgency later.

It was Ann who discovered Diana in the kitchen, almost doubled over the sink whilst she made the coffee.

'Marcus! Michael!' she called out anxiously, her practised eye taking in the situation at a glance.

Both men came running.

'Diana's gone into labour,' Ann told them. 'Marcus, bring round the car.'

'No!' Diana shook her head, trying to breathe deeply.

'Diana, don't be a fool,' Marcus told her grimly. 'I know you've got this bee in your bonnet about having the baby here, but ...'

Between gritted teeth Diana told him bravely, 'It's too late for hospital ... there won't be time.'

A long look passed between them, and Ann, who had been timing her now visible contractions, interrupted briskly.

'Diana's right.'

'My God, you must have *known*,' Marcus was standing beside her and looking at her with a narrowed, despairing expression, and she couldn't lie. She *had* known—almost from the moment she got back to the farm. Her waters had broken ages ago, and all through dinner the contractions had strengthened.

'It's too late for arguments,' Ann interrupted firmly. 'Michael, how much difference is there between delivering a baby and delivering a calf?'

'Not much,' Michael told her, with a grin for Marcus's bewildered expression. 'You go and ring Dr Thomas, there's a good chap. Diana, can you manage to get upstairs?'

She could and did ... perfectly content now that she knew her child was going to be born at home where she had wanted it to be born.

The midwife and Dr Thomas arived just in time to see Marcus holding his daughter for the first time, a look of dazed wonder on his face.

Afterwards when the three of them were finally alone, Marcus looked challengingly at his wife and asked, 'You never intended to have her in hospital, did you? You're one stubborn and determined lady, Mrs Simons. I suppose I should have known *that* from the moment you invaded my hotel room and seduced me.'

'*I* seduced *you*?' Diana protested indignantly. 'I like that!'

'So did I!'

She laughed weakly. 'Oh Marcus, you make me so happy. I love you so much.'

She reached out for his hand and together they looked at their sleeping daughter.

'You've given me so much. You've given me back my faith in life and in love. I'm not afraid any more.' She held out her arms to him. 'What are we going to call her?'

He looked down at the sleeping child and then at her. 'Leslie?' he suggested quietly.

'Yes ...'

The baby stirred, and the poignancy of the moment was lost beneath their shared wonderment in the small daintiness of her.

Life went on, grief dimmed and faded; that was the natural order of things, and now, in addition to one another, they had this new life to cherish and love. She had been given so much, Diana thought gratefully. So very, very much. Out of great pain had come great love, and she would never cease being thankful for it.

Harlequin Temptation dares to be different!

Once in a while, we Temptation editors spot a romance that's truly innovative. To make sure *you* don't miss any one of these outstanding selections, we'll mark them for you.

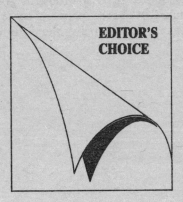

EDITOR'S CHOICE

When the "Editors' Choice" fold-back appears on a Temptation cover, you'll know we've found that extra-special page-turner!

THE

Temptation

EDITORS

Harlequin American Romance

Romances that go one step farther...
American Romance

Realistic stories involving people you can relate to and care about.

Compelling relationships between the mature men and women of today's world.

Romances that capture the core of genuine emotions between a man and a woman.

Join us each month for four new titles wherever paperback books are sold.
Enter the world of American Romance.

Harlequin Presents

Coming Next Month

Available in February wherever paperback books are sold, or through Harlequin Reader Service:

In the U.S.
901 Fuhrmann Blvd.
P.O. Box 1397
Buffalo, N.Y. 14240-1397

In Canada
P.O. Box 603
Fort Erie, Ontario
L2A 5X3

Keepsake

 Harlequin Books

You're never too young to enjoy romance. Harlequin and Keepsake, young-adult romances, destined to win hearts, for your daughter.

Pick one up today and start your daughter on her journey into the wonderful world of romance.

Two new titles to choose from each month.